L O S T

JACQUELINE DAVIES

LOST

MARSHALL CAVENDISH

Marshall Cavendish Corporation, 99 White Plains Road,
Tarrytown, NY 10591
www.marshallcavendish.us/kids
Library of Congress Cataloging-in-Publication Data

Davies, Jacqueline, 1962-
Lost / by Jacqueline Davies.
p. cm.
Summary: In 1911 New York, sixteen-year-old Essie Rosenfeld
must stop taking care of her irrepressible six-year-old sister when
she goes to work at the Triangle Waist Company, where she
befriends a missing heiress who is in hiding from her family and
who seems to understand the feelings of heartache and grief that
Essie is trying desperately to escape.
ISBN 978-0-7614-5535-6
[1. Grief—Fiction. 2. Loss (Psychology)—Fiction. 3. Sisters—
Fiction. 4. Immigrants—Fiction. 5. Arnold, Dorothy Harriet
Camille, b. 1884?—Fiction. 6. Triangle Shirtwaist Company—Fire,
1911—Fiction. 7. Jews—United States—Fiction. 8. New York
(N.Y.)—History—1898-1951—Fiction.] I. Title.
PZ7.D29392Lo 2009
[Fic]—dc22

2008040560

"That's Why I Wasn't Surprised, " from The Last Time I Saw
Amelia Earhart by Gabrielle Calvocoressi. Copyright © 2005.
Reprinted by permission of Persea Books, Inc. (New York)

Book design by Anahid Hamparian
Editor: Margery Cuyler

Printed in TK
First edition
1 3 5 6 4 2
mc Marshall Cavendish

Acknowledgments

It took me ten years to figure out how to tell the story of the Triangle Shirtwaist Factory Fire. Along the way, a lot of people offered me encouragement, editorial advice, and stores of knowledge. I'd like to thank them here, though I have already blessed every one of them in my heart.

Thank you to every member of the Monday Night Newton Writers Group who read the first few chapters of the first draft of this book in 1999. In particular, I want to acknowledge the leader of that group, Ruth Landers Glass, who passed away in 2005. Ruth was an unflagging cheerleader of my work. She shared with me stories of her mother's youth on Hester Street and helped spur me on at a time when I was feeling most tentative about this story.

Thanks to my tireless readers and jolly writer friends: Mary Atkinson, Tracey Fern, Jennifer Jacobson, Sarah Lamstein, Carol Peacock, and Dana Walrath. How many times did they read this book for me? We've all lost count. Without their insight and camaraderie, this book would never have been completed.

I received enormous help from the knowledgeable docents and staff at the Lower East Side Tenement Museum. In particular, I want to thank Sarah Pharaon, Director of Education, and David Favaloro, Research Manager, for pointing me in the direction of others who could answer my questions. Helene Tuchman, retired librarian at the Rabbi Marshall R. Lifson Library of Temple Emanuel of Newton, Massachusetts, and Murray Tuchman, retired director of the Hebrew College Library, both read the manuscript and shared with me their in-depth knowledge of the historical and cultural setting of my story. Likewise, Annie Polland, Vice-President for Education at the Museum at Eldridge Street, took the time to read the manuscript and offered me her wisdom. I am eternally grateful to these kind people. Any inaccuracies in the book are entirely my responsibility.

I send heartfelt thanks to Gabrielle Calvocoressi for writing the poem that helped me understand what my book was about and for allowing me to include a short excerpt as this book's epigraph.

As I traveled the long road to finishing this story, Margery Cuyler appeared like a guardian angel at a point when I thought I couldn't take even one more step. She scooped me up and offered to help me cross the finish line. Along the way, she asked important questions and supported me in my efforts to find answers to them. Most critically, she asked, "What would happen if Harriet worked in the factory alongside Essie?" That question spun the book in a different direction, and for that, I am so very thankful.

Every book I write owes some of its life to my agent Tracey Adams. This book in particular required more hand-holding than usual. What can I say? Tracey, I love ya.

And finally, how did my family put up with me as I worked my way through the endless writer's cycle of work, elation, despair? They are champions of forbearance and awfully nice folks to come home to. Many thanks to you—Mae, Henry, Sam, and John—hearts of my heart.

To
Margery Cuyler,
who proved her faith

And in memory of
Ruth Landers Glass
(1929-2005)
friend, mentor, and descendant of the Lower East Side
who read an early draft of this book and was the first to
say, "keep going"

That's why I wasn't surprised

when that woman got lost.
Because it's always like that.
One day, walking through a room,

you realize what you were holding
is gone and you can't find it, even
when you get down on your knees.

From "The Last Time I Saw Amelia Earhart"
a poem by Gabrielle Calvocoressi

February 6, 1905

Mama is on the bed grunting like a pig, and Ida Pelz from next door is telling her to push. This is the fifth time Mrs. Pelz has helped Mama get a baby out. The first two times brought me, then Saulie. The last two times brought nothing but grief.

Saulie is in school, unless he's hooking, like he does most days. I should be in school, too, but clever me, I told Mama that my ear ached, and so she let me stay home.

And don't you see how God works in this world? Such a little lie it was, but this, this is my punishment. Standing in this dark hole of a room while Mama's insides spill onto the bed. I'm just ten years old, I shouldn't see any of this, but there is no one else to help. And Mrs. Pelz, she needs the hands.

The *farshtinkener* room brings up my breakfast. I spit into the bowl that's on the bedside table and then dump the mess into the kitchen slop sink. Before I'm even done, Mrs. Pelz is calling me back, back into the bedroom. She needs me to push Mama's shoulders from behind, push her up like I could squeeze the baby right out of her. I climb behind Mama on the bed. I'm tall and strong for my age, but the vomiting has left me emptied out and weak-feeling. And Mama is like a sack of coal, heavy and all broken to pieces.

Mrs. Pelz is worried, I can tell. She keeps muttering under her breath, words from her village outside Bialystok. She's a greener, like Mama is,

1

like Papa was. But me, I was born in this America, so I don't know her strange words from a village far away, where they burn Jews just for being Jews. I only know the East Side of New York, where they don't let people burn.

But I know what she is thinking on, Mrs. Pelz. She is thinking on the last two babies. A boy, then two years later a girl, both born silent and blue, buried on the days they were born. The boy, my father named Daniel, which means God is my judge. The girl, he named Miriam, which means sea of bitterness.

But Papa is not here today. Eight months now, dead and buried. I am here, and Mrs. Pelz is here, and we are thinking on those babies. My hands are shaking and my breath won't come like it should. I don't know what Mama is thinking. She is grunting like a pig, and I don't know what pigs think.

Mrs. Pelz wants this baby to come fast, and she tells Mama to push. "Push, Hannah, push!" Mama does, and then there is a sound, a sucking, squeezing, splash of a sound, like water dumped in the slop sink. She screams, Mama does, one last time, and throws herself back on top of me so hard I flatten like shoe leather. Mama moans and rolls over onto her side, turning away from me, turning her back to me. I scramble off the bed like it's jumping with fleas.

Mrs. Pelz is holding a slippery mess. Gray and yellow, smeared with blood, and covered in a cloudy skin, it looks like something you'd pull out from under a wagon wheel.

But it isn't blue.

And it isn't silent.

The baby screams, a throaty, jagged sound that shreds my heart into pieces.

"*Gott sei dank!*" Mrs. Pelz announces, and snips the cord with her heavy iron scissors, the ones she uses to cut the skin off a chicken.

"Essie!" she says. "Fetch the water," and I fetch the basin that is warming near the stove. Mrs. Pelz washes the baby and gives her a rubber nipple to suck, then wraps her in a torn square of blanket that we saved special on the high shelf in the cupboard where we keep the Shabbat candlesticks. "Such hair!" she says, laughing as the black spikes bristle under her hand. "She is strong!"

But to me she looks as weak as a dream, shriveled and helpless. Mama has hardly eaten these past eight months, and I wonder that the baby could grow at all inside her. I reach out my hand and one of the baby's fists knocks into mine.

"Hannah," Mrs. Pelz says, walking to the head of the bed. "Only look, Hannah Rosenfeld, at the beauty of this child." But Mama won't look. She is curled on her side, her face buried in her pillow. She will not look at that baby.

Mrs. Pelz considers Mama, and then steps away from the bed. "*Nu*, some soup," she says. "And a taste of bread. A little something on the tongue to bring back the strength." She walks over to me before heading to the kitchen and hands me the heavy warm blanket that is my sister, and I reach out my arms and take her, take all of her—and she is mine.

Chapter 1

THE NEW GIRL WAS LOST. ANYBODY COULD SEE THAT.

I looked up from my machine to see her coming down the last aisle, behind Mrs. Gullo, and right off I could tell she'd taken a wrong turn, ended up in the wrong place, and was trying to figure out how to get back. I watched her look over her shoulder, and her face when it turned to me said, *Give me a minute, I'm making a plan.*

Or maybe she wasn't lost, but she'd lost *something*. She kept looking down at the factory floor, her eyes darting back and forth like sparrows on a roof's edge, and then turning around to check behind her. And just before she got to Molly's empty chair, which is right across the table from mine at the very end of the last aisle, she gave her skirts a shake, like she thought something might fall out.

I knew that feeling! How many times, in just the last week, I'd had that feeling. Something was here, just here, wasn't it? I'd look at my hands, slap the pockets of my skirt. What was it? What did I misplace? Did I put something down and forget to pick it up? Where did I leave it? *Oy!* I hated that nagging feeling, that poking thought circling the edge of my brain.

The new girl reached a nervous hand up to her throat and fiddled with the lace at her neck.

LOST

Something lost. I touched a finger to the bruise on my forehead above my right eye. It was almost gone, faded to a thin yellow. Hardly you could see it anymore.

I felt good-heart Freyda next to me nudge her foot against mine under the table. Her way of saying, *Look what's coming down the aisle.* I nudged back, *Yes, I see.*

Freyda, she was my best friend. Heart of my heart, we grew up side by side on Orchard Street. But I almost never saw her anymore. Too busy! So many things to do. Always I had to keep moving.

We used to walk to work together every day — was it just a week ago I had all the time in the world? — but now, I was up and out of the flat before the sun even cracked the sky. With all the errands, the shopping, the housework still to do, I didn't have time to chatter. At the end of the day, when the factory bell rang and all the girls stood up from their machines and stretched their arms and put a hand on their sore backs, Freyda always tried to get my eye. She wanted us to hook arms and walk home together, talking ourselves out to each other like we did before. But me, I had to get going. Out the door. Into the market. Always hunting for the bargain that would save a penny. Where to find hat trimmings I could afford? Who had the best price on taffeta, buckram, framing wire? To find these bargains took time. I never stopped. From the moment I woke up until I crawled into bed late at night, I never stopped. Then I was so tired, I would fall straight into sleep.

I wondered if Freyda understood that it just couldn't be like it was before.

To tell the truth, sometimes I thought Freyda was going maybe a little crazy. She said the strangest things sometimes. I wouldn't want to be crazy in the air like that.

"You!" Mrs. Gullo shouted over the noise of the machines, slapping her knotted rope on the tabletop. "Essie Rosenfeld!" I stood up. None of the other girls stopped their work. Not one. We got paid to sweat, not to watch a new girl take her seat, and if Mrs. Gullo caught any one of us gawking, she'd dock us a dime just for the look.

She was in a foul mood, Mrs. Gullo. Molly's chair had been empty since yesterday when Molly fainted in her seat and had to be carried out. Then Molly didn't show up for work this morning, which meant she might as well not come back at all. Mrs. Gullo wasn't going to keep a chair empty, waiting for some girl to get her strength back. Mrs. Gullo didn't like empty chairs. Empty chairs meant less money in her pocket at the end of the week, and The Bull loved money more than she loved God. She jutted a stubby thumb in the direction of the new girl. "Show her the ways."

I nodded my head. *Oy, gevalt.* This was the third girl I'd trained this month, and me, still new myself. I'd only been in the shop for eight weeks, but—my own fault—I'd shown that I could teach a new girl *and* keep up with my own work. Stupid. I'd been showing off, and look what it got me.

Then Freyda stood up. Little Freyda. Good-heart Freyda, her hands grabbing onto her own skirt to keep them from shaking. "Mrs. Gullo," she said, her voice thin and quivery, "Essie can't. She's in mourning."

Now, why would she say that? What would make her say such a thing? This craziness of Freyda's, it made me so angry. It was all I could do to keep my hands at my side. They felt like they wanted to fly right up and strangle that Freyda. Strangle those crazy words of hers so that they died in her throat.

"*Hush*, Freyda," I said, my lips pressed together, my hands balled up to keep them still. I felt a tightness in my chest, like someone was squeezing my rib cage. Good Freyda. Heart of my heart. My best friend since I could walk. I could feel the blood throbbing in my hands. If she said another word, even one more word of her craziness, I would have to take my fist and shove it down her throat, stuffing her words back inside her so they'd never come up —*black, ugly things* — again.

"It's true," said Freyda, looking back and forth from Mrs. Gullo to me, like a scared jackrabbit what is cornered by a fox. "Even though she don't show it. Her sister Zelda —"

"Shut up!" I said. "Don't you say!" I took a step forward, and Freyda stumbled back, away from me —afraid —and fell into her chair. She looked at me with a wildness in her eyes —crazy, I'm telling you, it almost broke my heart to see it —then she dropped her head and looked down at her hands in her lap.

"My sister's fine," I said, turning to Mrs. Gullo.

"Essie, please," whispered Freyda, not looking up.

Mrs. Gullo swung the knotted rope, smacking it onto the table. It made the sound of a gunshot, and I saw a few girls jump, but nobody looked up. "You!" she shouted at Freyda, "get back to work!" And Freyda did, because The Bull holds our lives in her hands, and if she squeezes too hard, we die.

"Show her the ways," Mrs. Gullo growled at me. Then she turned and stumped back up the aisle, leaving the new girl standing like a corner lamppost.

I turned and got my first good look at her. She was short and thick in the middle, shaped like a barrel stuffed with herring. Her face was wide and round as a dinner plate, and she had a tangle of chestnut hair twisted up under her hat. I couldn't tell how old she was. Twenty? Maybe not so old as that. Maybe older? It was hard to tell with her face looking like that—shifting and unsteady, like she was going to cry at any minute.

She was dressed nice, though. She had a proper coat, gray wool and sturdy-made. On her hands, tan walking gloves, which none of the girls wore on regular workdays. She carried a little purse, a velvet drawstring pouch that hung from her wrist, and she had a handkerchief in one hand. I thought, *I'll tell Zelda about that purse.* Zelda liked things, small things that you could pull closed or snap shut. Little boxes, small bags, anything with a snap or a latch or a drawstring. When you're six, you like things small.

LOST

The new girl was turning the purse in her hand. She was holding onto her handkerchief—it looked damp and a little dirty—and she was squeezing the purse like she was trying to feel for something inside.

"You lose something?" I asked.

"My key . . . I think . . . I think I might have lost the key to my apartment. It was here, I'm almost certain, in my purse, but then I took out my handkerchief and now it's gone. The key, I mean. I have a *bad habit* of losing keys." The whole time she said this, she was fumbling with her purse, and her eyes kept jumping from one place to the other—from her purse to my face to the floor and then back again, like she was caught on a carousel and couldn't get off.

"Well, you don't need it now," I said. "When you get home, someone will let you in."

"No, no," she said, digging into her purse and dropping her handkerchief onto the floor. "There's no one there. It's the second key I've lost already. The landlord will be angry."

I was about to say, "That's nothing compared to what Mrs. Gullo's going to be if you're not at your machine in the next ten seconds"—but I never got the chance. The new girl bent over to get her handkerchief, and when she stood up, she fainted. Her eyes looked up to the ceiling and the color fell off her face and her legs turned to twigs and crumpled up.

I caught her before she hit her head on the table, lucky for her, but let me tell you it was close. There's not much room on the shop floor—they have us packed in like sardines—and if you fall, you're going to hit *something* on the way down. She went down like a ton of bricks, the new girl. I heaved her onto my chair and flopped her head between her legs, and Freyda peeled off her gloves, which can pinch the circulation, and started to slap her hands to get the blood back in her. It was a good thing The Bull still had her back to us, or else she would have seen everything, and that new girl would have been out on the street.

She came to in seconds. *Eh*, it was just a little faint.

"Did you have breakfast?" I asked her when her eyes stopped spinning. She shook her head. "Well, dinner break isn't for an hour, so you'll have to hold on. Can you?" She nodded. "Here, lean on me," I said, "but don't make it look like you are." I glanced up the aisle at Mrs. Gullo's back. We worked our way around the crowded end of the table. I had to kick two workbaskets out of the way — the floor of the shop is always crammed with junk — and then I put her down in her own chair, the one right opposite mine.

"Give me your things," I said. I took her coat and her purse and her hat. Freyda handed me her gloves.

It was a nice hat. And let me tell you, I know from hats. It was one of those crushed Pamelas done up in winter velvet with a spray of gold seeding on the brim. A hat like that can spruce a girl up, make her shine, even in a factory. But that new girl, there was nothing about her that shined. She was lost, right from the minute she walked in.

I hung her things up on a nail on the wall behind her chair. There wasn't time to go to the coatroom and hang her things in a locker. Me? I never bothered with that. I hung my own things on a nail by the window because who's got time to *schlep* all the way to the coatroom at closing time? Two hundred and forty girls all trying to get their hats and coats and bags at once. It could take an hour just to get your things and get out the door. A girl could grow old and die waiting that long.

When I turned back, Yetta Goldstein in the next seat over was handing the new girl a bit of a dried-up roll. Yetta always kept a little something in her pocket, just in case. She was a big girl, and sometimes you needed a little something. The new girl put the crust in her mouth and let it sit on her tongue without chewing it. Her face was gray, and her lips were yellow, and she looked like she might throw up. She lifted her eyes and said, "I'm sorry to cause trouble." Her voice, it was thin as straw. I could have reached out with two fingers and snapped that voice in half.

I waved her apology away. There wasn't time for such things. If that new girl didn't have a finished waist in her basket by the noon bell, her job wasn't worth a sour pickle.

"So, we begin," I said.

I moved behind her seat, and then that girl did such a queer thing. She held out her hand and said, "My name is Harriet Abbott." Just like that. Like I was a Carnegie and she was a Rockefeller and we were at the social event of the season.

I frowned and shook my head. Then I pointed to the machine. "We don't get paid for talking." *Oy, vey iz mir*, I felt in my heart again that sinking feeling. This new girl wouldn't last the day. What was the point?

She turned and put her hands on the table, then she looked up at me, waiting. I could see that her hands were smooth and soft, not one scar or patch of rough skin. On her wedding finger, she wore a thin ring that looked like it was made of tin. *Gott im himmel!* Every move she made told me she had never been in a factory. This was pointless! Already I could feel the girls in my row getting ahead. Mrs. Gullo would give me a piece of her rope if I didn't keep up.

"Press the pedal to see how it feels," I said, resting my hands on her shoulders and bending over to guide her. "It's a pull, so be careful you don't get yourself caught up in the belt." I'd seen that once, a girl's leg burned so bad she had to go to the hospital.

The new girl pressed the pedal, and I could feel a shiver of fear run through her. The needle on her machine jigged up and down, and she pulled back as if it might reach out and bite her. *Good*, I thought. *Fear is a good thing in a factory.*

I pointed to the wicker basket on the floor next to her. "These are your pieces. They're cut by the *shlemiels* on the eighth floor. Some are cut good, some are cut not so good. But you've got to make every piece work. You can't send pieces back just 'cause they're cut by a chimp."

LOST

The new girl picked up a piece and fingered the fabric. It was lawn—stiff, white, woven cotton, more like paper than cloth and harder to work with. I could see that she was gauging its stretch and give, which is good, because it meant she knew a thing or two about material. She had a feel.

"First you sew the placket," I said. "It's marked at the notches, here and here. Three inches long. No longer than that. We don't put on the cuffs. Those come later, so leave the end raw. When you're done with that, give me a sign and I'll show you what's next."

"Thank you," she said softly. "Thank you so very much." Like she was a Rockefeller! Again, I waved away her words. There wasn't time for please and thank you in the shop.

I moved back to my seat and set to work on the sleeve that hung from my machine. It's not good to stop a seam midway. It always feels broken, no matter how carefully you line it up. I pressed my foot to the pedal and felt the belt hook onto the drive axle. My needle jumped and I leaned in.

I was deep into it, in that place where my eyes and hands become part of the machine, a place of forgetting, which is the only way to sew, really— when I saw the new girl out of the corner of my eye. Her hand fluttered near her head and I could see she was trying to get my attention. I stood up and went to her machine to check her work.

"What's this?" I asked, pointing at the piece. It hadn't been touched. Five minutes had gone by and she hadn't sewn a stitch.

13

"I don't know how to thread the machine," she said. "I tried it three different ways, but I couldn't get it right. Could you possibly show me how?"

"You don't know—? How did you get in here?" I asked. I didn't mean to make her cry, but the girl was taking up my time, and I was the one who'd pay for it.

Her chin began to tremble and her eyes got wet. Suddenly, she looked so young. Younger even than Saulie. As young as Zelda. A little girl lost on Delancey. She was trying her hardest not to cry, but the tears were coming anyway. Her hand began to fuss with the cheap lace collar around her neck. There was a thread loose, and her nervous fingers started to tug at it.

"Stop," I said, swatting her hand like I do when Zelda fusses with a dress I'm fitting on her. "Come here. I can fix that." She leaned closer to me and I wrapped the loose string twice around my index finger and snapped it off. Then I tucked the short end inside her collar.

The girl looked down at her hands in her lap. A thread of tears ran down each cheek. "I can sew," she said, her voice low. "Really I can. I just don't know how to thread the machine."

"Look, New Girl, I don't know where you come from," I said. "But you won't last a day here. Mrs. Gullo is going to check your work, and she'll have you out on the street—through the window if you won't leave by the door."

"I can do this," she said, mashing her tears

roughly with the heel of her hand. "And I need this job. Please?"

Oy! Gott im himmel. "Watch," I said, not wanting to waste another second arguing. Using my elbow, I pushed her over and threaded the machine quick. I have good eyes and fast fingers, and I've been threading since I was four.

"Thank you—" she said, but I didn't wait to hear more. I was behind, and if I didn't have twenty finished waists in my basket by the lunch hour, Mrs. Gullo would throw me out on the street, just for the fun of it.

Five minutes later, the new girl showed me a nice placket. Neat, square, the right length. She'd taken the time to trim her own threads, though.

"It's okay," I said, "but it took you too long. You'll have to go twice as fast if you want to keep your chair."

She nodded, her face serious. "I'll get faster. There's—"

I held up my hand. "We're not allowed to talk. We'll get docked if we do. Just finish the sleeve. Straight up the seam to the underarm, then set it in the bodice. And *don't* trim your own threads. Just leave 'em hanging."

I sat down in my chair and leaned over to Freyda, who turned her ear to catch my words. "The new girl needs help. Tell Ida." The three of us were fast. Together, we could pull the new girl through today.

Tomorrow, she was on her own.

When The Bull came charging down the aisle

to inspect the work in the new girl's basket, she found four finished waists. Three were done expertly. One had the smallest pucker at the back of one shoulder.

"No good," said The Bull, shoving the bad one in the new girl's face.

"I'm sorry," said the new girl. "It was my first. The rest are better."

"This one! This one comes out of your pay," said Mrs. Gullo, shaking the shirtwaist like a drowned cat. But she took it with her, instead of throwing it on the floor for scrap, which meant she would try to pass it off to Mr. Bernstein, who was the production manager. The sleeve was close to good enough. She might slip it by him and get paid for it.

When the closing bell rang and the machines went dead, I stood up along with all the other girls. What a noise! You keep that many girls quiet all day, they just about explode with the talking.

I felt a hand on my arm. Freyda, looking at me with those big eyes. Before she could even ask, I was explaining myself away. "*Oy!* So much to do tonight, with all the errands. I'll see you tomorrow, okay, Freyda?"

But she didn't let go. Little Freyda. The top of her head barely reached my chin. So small I could tuck her in my coat pocket and not even know she was there. "Essie, tonight maybe, why don'cha come home?"

I frowned and shook my head. "I can't. I wish I

could. I'm looking for feathers. Old, used ones. For Zelda's hat. Something I can trim down and make look good. I still haven't finished. And her birthday, already a month ago." I shook my head again. "I can't."

The feathers were the least of it. I still hadn't found the silk cheap enough to cover the enormous frame of the hat. When you're poor, you have to shave the pennies off of everything you buy. Tonight, I would spend all evening in Chinatown haggling with the yellow men to get the organdy a penny cheaper a yard. This hat, this ridiculous Merry Widow hat for Zelda, was going to cost me everything I had.

I patted Freyda's hand on my arm, then lifted it off me and stepped away. I slipped around the end of the table, as if I had something to say to the new girl. Then it was easy to get away. The long table was between me and Freyda, and I already had my hat and shawl in my hands. Freyda had her eyes on me, but what could she do? Lock me up in a room? Lock me in a room without windows? What could she do?

I shouted, "G'night, Freyda," and started to shove my way up the last aisle. Let the other girls think I'm pushy. Let them say I'm rude. I had to get out. There were so many things I had to do. I wouldn't get home until late, long after Mama and Zelda and even Saulie were in bed. They would be sleeping, and I would slip in like the fog. In the morning, I'd be gone before light.

The girls didn't give me dirty looks, though. They just moved aside and let me go past. It's like I passed through them, like I was a ghost made of nothing but mist. Not one of them looked at me, and I wondered if I was turning invisible. I'd been feeling that way all week. It seemed to me that people never looked *right at me* anymore. They were always looking to the side of me or behind me or above me, like I wasn't really there. With one hand, I delicately touched my face. Was it fading away?

Out on the street, I pulled my shawl tighter and headed into the March night. Snow had fallen during the day, and the evening world was silver and glistening. I would head straight south down Lafayette to Canal, right into the heart of Chinatown, where nobody knew me and nobody asked any questions. Down Mulberry, up Mott, I would poke into every single silk shop until I found what I was looking for. Sometimes I got lucky on these bargain hunts. But it took time. That's the thing about shopping for the good bargains. You had to be patient. Me, I was patient.

But Zelda wasn't. She would be mad, I knew this. Mad because I didn't stay home with her anymore. Mad because I went to the shop so early every morning and didn't come home until she was already asleep. Mad because we couldn't play hide-and-seek the way we used to. *Oh, it's you!*

She would probably be so mad the next time I saw her that she would find a hiding place and not come out for hours. Just to punish me. That's what she did—she hid, and I could never find her!

LOST

But she must know: it was all for her! *When I give her the hat, she'll forgive me,* I told myself. I knew this in my heart, so I held that feeling close to me and hurried through the snow.

February 27, 1905

Mama gets up out of bed. It's been three weeks since the baby was born, three weeks since Mama left the bedroom except to go to the toilet. Her hair is snarled and matted down her back. Her nails are long. Her skin looks like old cheese.

I have been rocking the baby, settling her down to sleep, singing a lullaby in Yiddish that Mama used to sing to me: *In dem Beis-Hamikdosh, In a vinkl cheyder . . .*

> *In the room of the temple,*
> *In a cozy corner,*
> *There sits a widow all alone.*

I stare at Mama as she walks into the kitchen, like I'm seeing the ghost of someone I used to know. She has pulled on a skirt and a blouse. The blouse is wrinkled and untucked in the back. The third button down is missing, leaving an embarrassing gap that makes me think of an old woman's smile.

The baby is asleep in my arms, drunk on milk. Sophie Lasky said she'd nurse her if I paid her a dollar a week. I have no idea how I'll get the money, but I said yes. What could I do? The baby screams when she's hungry, a cry that's like a knife to my heart. So now I walk down to the third floor a dozen times a day to feed the baby. We just got back, and now Mama is up on her feet and moving around with a purpose.

"Good morning, Mama," I say. I wonder if she'll ask me why I'm not in school. Has she even noticed that I haven't gone since the baby was born? The truant officer came pounding on the door yesterday—ten-year-olds have to go to school, it's the law—but me and the baby hid in the blanket box and Mama slept straight through.

Mama looks at me and makes a low growl deep in her throat, "*Mmmm.*" Nothing more. She pulls a chair over to the high cupboard and climbs on top of it. From the high shelf, she takes down the *Shabbos* candlesticks, the ones that are made of poor man's brass but that have been in her family for three generations. *The gift of a gift of a gift.* They are heavy in her hands, like weights she has to carry. She sets them on the table. Then she opens the top drawer of the cupboard and takes out the white linen tablecloth and the set of four embroidered napkins we use only for the Shabbos meal. Finally, she opens the door of the cupboard and takes down the pewter kiddush cup, engraved with the tree of life, that was given to them by Papa's family when they married. The pewter is dull. I haven't polished it for nearly a month now. I wonder if she's angry at me for this. Her face looks angry, clouded over and pinched at the corners of her mouth.

"Take these," she says to me. "Take them to Reb Elias's shop. Get what you can for them. Don't take his first offer, remember that. Never take his first offer."

I look at her, not understanding. "Mama, we can't sell these things. How will you say the prayers? How will we set the table?"

Mama disappears into the back bedroom. When she comes out, she is carrying Papa's *tallis*, the prayer shawl he wore to *shul* each morning. The shawl is white with blue and silver embroidery near the edges. It's folded carefully, just as he left it. I haven't seen it for eight months, and it makes my throat choke closed, just the sight of it.

She places the white shawl carefully on the table and smooths it once before saying, "This, too."

"No, Mama! Not Papa's *tallis*. That will go to Saulie when he's old enough."

Mama looks at me through narrow eyes. Her voice is a thin razor. "You will disobey me? Take them. We have another mouth to feed." She latches the cupboard door, closes the drawer, then runs her hand along the tabletop and sees the dust there.

I can't believe she's telling me to sell these things. It's like she's telling me to sell our faith—*and get the best price you can for it.*

"What would Papa say?" I ask. "He would *never* want you to sell these things."

"Don't," says Mama, warning me.

"He wouldn't. Papa would say—"

Mama puts both hands flat against her temples and screams. She presses her hands as though her head will fall to pieces. She looks up to the ceiling and cries, "Why are you doing this to me?"

I don't know if she's asking me or Papa or God. It doesn't much matter. Nobody answers.

"Mama," I say quietly. "We will need these things. Now that you've got your strength back. We will need to set the table. We will need to light the candles."

"No," says Mama, dropping her hands. "We will never need these things again. Take them and sell them. The money, we can use. These things, these are nothing to me." She turns to go back into the bedroom.

It frightens me to hear her talk like this. "Mama, stop," I say. "You—" I can't think what else to say. I want to hold her in the room. I want her to put back the candlesticks, smooth the *tallis* and return it to its drawer. I want her to look at the baby, just *once*. She has never rested her eyes on the baby—not even one time. I hold the baby out. "You have to give her a name," I say at last.

The baby breathes in sharply and then lets out a long, shuddery sigh. I've been holding her for nearly half an hour and suddenly she feels unbearably heavy.

Mama looks at me. "Papa named all the babies."

It's true. Papa gave us our names. Esther means *star*, and Papa said that's why I turned out so beautiful. I was named for Mama's grandmother, an old woman who died in Odessa when the massacres broke out in the spring of 1871.

Saulie was named for Papa's uncle, a rug merchant. He died defending his house against robbers that entered through an unlatched window in the middle of a moonless night. Saul means *one who was wanted*, as of course all firstborn sons are.

Birth and death — always, they exist side by side. The names of the dead are given to the newly born, so like threads in a cloth we are woven together.

But ever since Papa died, the cloth has been unraveling. Saulie, skipping school and hanging out on the wharves. Me, doing the take-in laundry on *Shabbos*. Mama, not even getting up to say the prayers these three weeks. What would Papa say? *What? Are you not even Jews anymore?* I can see him pounding his fist on the kitchen table, telling us who we are.

We are coming all undone. Mama most of all.

But here she is. She is up. She is out of bed. Maybe everything will be all right now?

She looks at the baby. Looks at her long and hard. I can't tell what she's thinking. I wait.

"You name her," she says, turning away. "I have to get myself ready. I need to find work." She walks into the back bedroom, closing the door behind her.

The baby turns her head, eyes still closed, and raises up her fine, thin eyebrows. Her lips part, and her mouth makes a pretty O. She looks like she might ask me a question. She looks like she might wake up. But then her tiny face relaxes and she settles back into heavy sleep.

I look at her, feel the heavy heat of her, and my heart rips in two. I look at her and I bury my face into the warm moist damp of her and nuzzle my lips up to her seashell ear and whisper, "Zelda. It means *luck*."

Chapter 2

THE STAIRWELL WAS DARK. THE STAIRWELL WAS always dark. No windows, no gas jets, and no moon tonight—just clouds and the threat of more snow. It was three long flights up to our flat, which was on the top floor. I put my foot on the first step and began to climb.

I was tired from combing the shops in Chinatown looking for black organdy at a price I could afford. I had been on my feet for hours, and I had nothing to show for it. It would take three yards to cover the umbrella-sized brim. That meant I needed to get lucky and find remnants that I could piece together, hiding the seam with the trimmings. (I was good at that trick.)

But tonight was not my lucky night.

Halfway up the first flight of stairs, I wondered if Zelda would come running down the way she did every night since I started working in the factory. She would have seen me from the fire escape—*how did I miss her there tonight?*—and soon I would hear the banging of her footsteps in the echoey stairwell as she rushed at me.

On the second-floor landing, I thought I could hear her coming, so I braced myself for the collision. I kneeled down and spread my arms out wide, so that through the darkness she could run at me and smash into me like a freight train on a straightaway going fifty miles an hour.

Just like she always did.

I would wrap my arms around her and feel the glorious weight of her, the solid thickness of her, the heavy *thereness* of her, and I would think, *I made this*. I made this girl so strong and healthy. The food I cooked, the baths I gave, the dresses I stitched and socks I mended. All those years of *taking care* grew this girl who was so strong and alive.

And then she would say, "You're late," with a stamp of her foot.

And I would say, "I know. Can you forgive me? The Bull made me stay extra." I would bury my nose in her hair, and the wondrous smell of it—of lemon and soap and Zelda—would make me faint dead away.

And then she would kiss me right on the lips and say very seriously, "I forgive you. But I hate that Mrs. Gullo!"

"Me, too!" I would say gleefully, and then stand up and take her hand and we would walk up the last two flights together, her telling me about her day: the morning spent at school and the afternoon with Mrs. Pelz, who watched her now that I worked in the factory.

I kneeled on the cold floor, wrapped up in the dark of the stairwell, and waited. She didn't come, and I thought, *Well, it's late. Of course she's in bed by now.* So I stood up, but in that dark so deep I couldn't even see my hand in front of my face, I thought again, *I must be going invisible. Slowly, I'm just fading away.* I waved my hand in front of my face, but there was nothing there.

I was still standing in the hallway, waving my own invisible hand in front of my face, when I heard the footsteps and a whistling coming up from below.

I turned on the landing so that I was facing back the way I'd come, and I stood still because I wanted to see if I really was invisible. Did I even have a body? What would happen if *his* body smashed into mine? Would he just pass through? Would he feel that he had walked right through me?

And I wanted—*yes*—I wanted his body to press into mine.

I had been dreaming about Jimmy Eagan for three years, ever since Mrs. Pelz took him in as a boarder when he started at the university. At first, when I was still just a little girl of twelve, I used to dream of walking in the park with him. And then, as I got older, I dreamed of holding hands with him. But now that I was sixteen, grown tall and looking to all the world like a woman (and a beauty, they say, the old women on stoops, who tell me my face will be my fortune, though I don't know anything about that), my dreams of Jimmy had become so shocking that I blushed in my bed at night.

When I imagined these things, my insides moved and melted and opened in a way I had never felt before, and I curled in on myself with a shame I couldn't name. To think such things was sinful, I knew. But I didn't want to stop.

I held my breath and waited for the crash.

But Jimmy was running his hand along the railing, the way you do in the dark, and he felt my hand resting there the second before he banged into me.

"Pardon me!" he said, taking a quick step back.

"It's me, Jimmy," I said.

"Essie? I didn't see you." He leaned forward, trying to get close enough to see my face in the darkness. "Can't see a damn thing. Someone's going to break his neck on these stairs. Hope it isn't me!" He let out a short laugh, then fell silent.

"Late class tonight?" I asked, leaning in to him. I wondered, if I accidentally pressed up against him, where would my lips fall? On his collar? The knot of his tie? His chest? I was tall, but he was taller. If he leaned down at just the right moment, would our lips accidentally meet? In the dark? On the stairs?

"Nah, I was out with friends," he said. "What about you? You're not just getting home from work, are you?" We were standing just a foot apart, and still I couldn't see anything of his face. I imagined the air between us—the clouded air filled with smells and dirt and the ghosts of all the people who have stood on these stairs—breaking up into tiny particles and falling away, one by one, until there was nothing left between us. Until, like magnets drawn together, we would be touching, the lengths of our bodies pressed together.

"Sort of," I said. "I stopped somewhere on the way home." I leaned in slightly, hoping he wouldn't notice, wanting to catch the smell of him. But the air was filled with the stink of fried potatoes and the toilets on the hallway. There was no way Jimmy's smell—coffee and soap and tobacco—could find me.

And then I felt his hand groping in the dark, trying to find my own hand on the railing. And when he did find it, when his fingers finally brushed mine, he lifted my hand and held it gently in both of his, and then he pressed it up to his heart and said, "The cemetery?"

My ears filled with buzzing, and I thought I might faint. I hadn't eaten anything since noon, and then only a slice of black bread and a pickle. It was the beginning of the month and there was always less to eat right after the rent got paid. Did I seem unsteady on my feet? Is that why Jimmy pulled me in closer? Is that why he put his hand on my back, like we were dancing? He was saying words, but the buzzing in my ears made me go deaf. The rough wool of my skirt brushed against the smooth cloth of his pants. Half an inch more and we would be pressed together, chest to chest, hip to hip, thigh to thigh. He was bending his head closer to mine now, and I could feel his breath on my cheek. If I turned my face up now, *just now*, would our lips meet?

His voice floated through the buzzing in my ears. ". . . I just wanted you to know that I loved her, too. We all loved her."

Love? He was whispering to me in the dark about love?

A door on the hall flew open and light flooded the landing. I jumped back from Jimmy. He dropped my hand. Mrs. Bornstein stood staring at us, her heavy hands on her hips. She could pick me up and pitch me over the railing if she wanted to. Jimmy too, I bet. I grabbed for the railing and started up the stairs, two at a time, Jimmy coming right behind me.

"G'night, Mrs. Bornstein," I shouted as I hurried up. I didn't even turn to Jimmy when I got to the top landing. My door was unlocked, so I threw it open and said, "G'night, Jimmy," tossing it over my shoulder before passing through. As I closed the door behind me, my first thought was, *Thank God Mama is already in bed.*

But she wasn't. There was a kerosene lamp burning in the back bedroom, and I could see into the room. Mama was there, up and dressed.

Quickly and as quietly as possible, I unlaced my boots and was about to put them on the clean square of newspaper Mama kept by the door when I noticed that Zelda's boots were gone. My heart jumped into my throat. Where were they? My brain started to spin, bringing back the headache that had been coming and going for a week now. I touched the soft yellow bruise over my eye. Where were Zelda's boots?

"Mama?" I called out, having trouble taking my eyes off the empty square of paper where Zelda's boots should have been. I walked into the bedroom.

Mama was standing by the bed. She had one of Zelda's dresses in her hands, the one with the yellow sash and the eyelet edging. The one I had made for her sixth birthday, just last month.

There were other dresses on the bed, too, along with her hats, the three smaller ones clustered around the skeleton frame of the Merry Widow hat I was still working on. That's when I noticed Zelda's boots. Mama had cleaned them off and put them on the chair beside the bed.

"What are you doing?" I asked.

Mama looked at me, her eyes tired. "Tell me," she said softly. "Tell me you know what I'm doing."

"I just made that dress," I said, pointing to the one in her hands. Mama knew this. "She's only worn it the once."

Mama pressed her lips together, then went back to her work. She shook the dress and pulled at a seam, looking for stains and rips. Then she put the dress on the bed. I could see now that there were two piles. She was sorting the clothes.

"Leave them," I said, feeling slightly panicked. "Why are you taking them down? Leave them!" Again, I felt that tightness in my chest, a weight pressing down on me. It was hard to pull in a breath.

"She always had too many dresses," said Mama, shaking her head. "Ridiculous, the way you made them every season. Nobody has such dresses her age."

"What are you doing?" I asked again.

"Her clothes, I'm getting rid of them. These we can sell. These go to the ragpicker."

"Have you gone crazy?" I rushed at her, snatching the dress from out of her hands. "Give me that dress. *I* made that dress. You can't give it away. You can't sell her clothes!"

Mama put her hands on her hips. She looked like she would fight me. I was taller than she was, but Mama was strong. What would she do? Tie me up and lock me in a room? Lock me in a room like I was an animal? Would she *really* do that?

"I won't have them anymore," she said quietly. She picked up one of Zelda's woolen stockings and stroked it with one hand. "They remind too much. They break my heart." Her fingers found a small hole in the knitting. She sighed, then put the stocking back on the bed. "And look. They take up half the room. Look at this!"

She flung her arms at the two coatracks and broken broom handle that I'd rigged up when Zelda's clothes wouldn't fit on hooks anymore. We called it Zelda's Dressing Room. The dresses, the hats, the costumes—I can make anything out of leftover scraps. It's my one talent, really—making something out of nothing.

"No!" I shouted. I grabbed up the clothes on the bed, messing up the piles, ruining Mama's work. "You can't do this. She needs these clothes. You can't just take her clothes away from her. What will she wear?"

"What will she wear, Essie? When?"

"When . . . when she comes back," I said. I wanted to run out of that room. I wanted to stop this talk. I wanted to hit Mama, hard, across the face. Anything to make her shut up.

"Back from where, Essie?" Mama's voice was sharp.

"From . . . wherever she is!" I shouted. "I don't

know exactly. Next door! Or in the front room! Maybe she's hiding in the hallway." I looked at the bed. The bed was empty. It was late at night. "I haven't looked everywhere. I can't watch her every second. I can't always know where she is."

"Enough, Essie!" snapped Mama. "Enough already with this crazy talk in the air."

"Don't you say!" I shouted. My voice was like a train whistle, warning anyone unlucky enough to get in my way. "Don't you say it!"

Mama made a move to push past me, to get at the clothes still hanging on the rack, but I blocked her with my whole body. She would have to flatten me to get at those clothes, and I was betting she couldn't do it. I pointed at the rack and looked her right in the face and said, "This is *not* happening."

Mama stopped and looked at me, hard. She was beyond exhausted. I knew she was having trouble sleeping these days. She shook her head. "This is craziness," she said. "You'll end up in the bug house if you go on like this." She stared at me, then threw her hands up in the air and let out a strangled sound that was half frustration, half disgust. "*Unh!*" Without another word, she walked out of the room.

Carefully, I put Zelda's boots on the square of newspaper by the front door. I hung up each dress, making sure to straighten the hems, flatten the buttons, smooth out any wrinkles. I checked, as Mama did, for any tears or holes. I found one seam that was weakening, beginning to pull apart, and I marked it with a pin. *I can fix that,* I said to myself. Tomorrow, I would make the repair.

June 26, 1906

"Oh, it's you!" I say, pulling my hands away from my face. Zelda squeals with delight, a gurgling coo that comes from deep inside her. A squeezed-up laugh held tight in the fist of her throat until it's finally let loose.

She claps her hands and grabs my wrists, pushing my hands back up to my face. So I cover my eyes again and say, "Who is it? Who is it? Who is there?" Then I wait, a good long time, because this is the part Zelda loves best. I can feel her bouncing up and down on my lap, so stuffed with joy that she can hardly hold it in.

Then I snap my hands open like two barn doors. "Oh, it's *you*!" I say, and Zelda makes that rising-falling scream that means that nothing in the world is better than this game.

It's June, hot, and the news is full of that man who got killed, that rich man at the theater last night. He was a famous architect and they say he built half of New York, but he's dead all the same. *Here, then gone.* Shot in the face, and all his money can't change that.

My legs have gone prickly under Zelda's weight, and my back is tight and angry from the hard kitchen chair, but I would play this game forever if I could. If there wasn't the laundry to finish and then supper to get on the table.

The latch on the door lifts, and Mama walks in. I'm caught off guard. I didn't expect her for another hour. Under her arm she's got a day-old loaf. The bakery pays her in wages and stale bread. I try to scuttle Zelda off my lap, but she grabs hold of my blouse and won't let go.

"You're early," I say, prying at Zelda's fingers that wrap like Coney Island seaweed around me.

Mama looks at us and then at the pile of clothes on the table waiting to go in the soak pot. "Put this in the cupboard," she says, handing me the bread. She reaches over and lifts Zelda off my lap. Zelda screams, and Mama says, "*Sha!*" giving her a little shake. The minute she's down, Zelda tries to climb back up.

"Essie, you don't let her," Mama warns, moving to the stove to check on the soaking clothes. "*Nu?* The water is cold. Why this is?"

I'm trying to peel Zelda off me and answer Mama's questions at the same time. "*Oy*, the weather, it's so hot, Mama. I hate to make the fire big."

"Whites need the hot. Nobody pays for clothes what are dingy. You did the bluing? It don't look like you blue'd 'em."

"I did, yeah, I did," I say, finally getting Zelda onto the floor by shaking her rag doll in front of her. The doll—Miss *Shpilkes*—I sewed from scraps begged off the rag peddler. Saulie named her when he saw me jabbing my needle in and out of her eyes, finishing the embroidery late one night.

I move over to the stove and take the paddle out of Mama's hands, poking the clothes in the pot. They'll need a second soak. Even I can see that.

"And these?" Mama asks, pointing to the pile on the table. She puts her hands on her hips. "What

35

have you been doing, Essie? Playing games? You and Zelda, playing games while I'm at work like a dog?"

"Only for a minute, Mama," I say.

"*Only for a minute,*" Mama mutters. "You spoil her, Essie. You give her too much the attention. It makes a child go soft and rotten. You'll see." Mama goes out of the flat and down the hall to use the toilet. I throw a scoop of coal on the fire and give the soaking clothes a good stir. Then I bend over, sticking my head under the kitchen table and whisper, "Oh, it's you!"

Zelda gurgles with delight, as I turn myself back to the stove and get to it.

Chapter 3

"COME HERE, I CAN FIX THAT," I SAID, STEPPING out of the shadow of the building into the feeble light of the corner gas lamp. Harriet—the new girl—was standing in the dull glow, pulling at the tie on her cloak. I could tell by the way she was tugging that she was only making it worse.

Girls from the factory poured out of the building. Closing time and everyone in a hurry to get home. They flowed past us like a river wild in the spring. I'd been stopping to retie my bootlace, bending down in the shadows in case Freyda appeared. I didn't want her coming with me, and I didn't want to explain to her why I felt that way. But now she'd gone past on her way home, and so it was safe to step into the light.

Harriet turned and looked at me and smiled. She let her hands drop limply to her side and lifted up her chin, the way a child would say, *I give up. You do it.*

I set to work on the knot. The light from the streetlamp was so weak I couldn't hardly see what I was doing. Mostly I let my fingers feel along the tangle of the tie to sense where it could be loosened.

"You did good today," I said. "You kept up with the worst." Three days in the shop, and the new girl was holding her own.

Harriet looked at me seriously, her chin lifted, her soft, white neck exposed to the night. She seemed to be trying to read my face, to figure out if I had just made a joke. "Is that a compliment?" she asked.

I nodded my head. "Yep, that's a compliment. And I don't give too many." I picked at the knot, using my nails, plucking and turning it, trying to find a spot that could be loosened. There didn't seem to be any. "How did you do this?" I asked, giving a little tug to find any slack.

"I don't even know," murmured Harriet. "I tied a knot and then a bow, but it seemed too tight around my neck, so I pulled on one of the ends and this is what happened."

"It's a good one, all right," I said. "But I can undo anything. *Any* mistake, I can fix it." We were silent then, and my fingers kept on working, turning the knot and feeling for the spot that would give way. There was always one. Harriet stared up at my face. The evening was chilly, and I could feel her warm breath settling on my hands, like a kitten that curls up against you to keep out the cold.

"That's a lovely hat," she said.

"Yeah? Thanks. I made it," I said, squinting in the dim light.

"Really? I'm impressed." She straightened up a bit to get a better look.

"Don't move," I said. "I've almost got it." The truth was, I was nowhere near finding the secret of that knot, but I didn't want her to know. It's like when I'm combing Zelda's hair and I tell her

38

"almost done" when there's still a huge tangle left.

"Sorry," she said. "It's quite fetching. Did you copy it?"

I smiled. She had an eye, all right. The hat had a day brim covered in brown taffeta and then sprigged with a single black plume that arched from the center of the crown to the back. In front, I'd ruched the ribbon hatband into an oversized bow and anchored it with a big buckle. It had taken me a month of crawling all over Chinatown to find taffeta like that I could afford. And the buckle I'd turned up in the ragpicker's pile, where he sells the scraps by the pound.

"No, I never copy, unless someone tells me, 'I want *that* hat,' and even then I make changes." Sewing I was good at, but making hats was my passion.

Harriet stared more sharply at the hat, appraising it. "You should go into business."

"Oh, I will," I said. "Well . . ." I shrugged my shoulders. "Someday. If I can save up the dough." I was always saving and Zelda was always spending! She liked things—ice cream cones, penny whistles, animal crackers, trips to the nickelodeon. Little things, really, when you thought about it, and I could never say no.

Harriet reached up and scratched her nose, delicately, with just the tip of her pinkie finger. I'd never seen anyone do like that, and I couldn't help but think, *Where does she come from?* Her mouth screwed up into a question. "What? Is it expensive? A hat shop?"

"A'course it is," I said. "Otherwise everyone would have one, wouldn't they? I mean, who would want to work for someone else if you could have your own shop?"

"Well, how much is it?" asked Harriet, her voice edged with impatience.

I shook my head and shrugged my shoulders again. "I don't know. I bet you'd need five hundred dollars. Maybe even more. Rent and materials and tools. And then, if you don't do good, you're sunk. All that money wasted, and your heart lost, too."

"Five hundred dollars," scoffed Harriet. "That's not so very much."

"*Huh!* It is where I come from!" I'd been trying to save for a year now, and all I had to show for it was twelve dollars and change. And if Mama ever found out about *that*, I'd have nothing to call my own. "*You* try saving out of what you make at the Triangle. You'll see."

Harriet nodded her head vigorously, short little sharp nods that snapped the knot right out of my hands. "I know!" she said. "It all goes so fast. You wouldn't think it would, but it does. A little here, a little there, and next thing you know there's nothing left in your purse!"

"Well, if there was, we'd all be shopkeepers, wouldn't we?"

She smiled then, and her eyes looked bright in the dim light. "Yes! We would. That would be fun, don't you think? We could have a shop together. Maybe hats and books. That would be nice."

Hats and books! I thought. *Who ever heard of such*

a queer thing? But I didn't say anything. This was nice, this conversation. For the first time in a week, I could just relax and say what was on my mind. I took in a deep breath. It was like breathing after you've been underwater for a long time.

I picked away at the knot. I was in no hurry.

But after another minute, Harriet got impatient. She shifted her weight from foot to foot. Her fingers fidgeted at her waistband.

"Maybe we should just cut it," she said, one of her hands crawling like a spider up her chest to give the tie a tug.

"What? Are you crazy?" I said, swatting her hand. "Then you have to sew the tie back on. Just be a little patient, would you? I swear, you're worse'n my little sister."

Harriet sighed and folded her arms across her chest, standing as still as a statue on a cold morning. "How old is *she*?"

"Six," I said. "And she has the patience of a flea. Look, see? I'm getting it now." I had found the weak spot in the knot—the place where, with a little coaxing, everything would come unraveled. I gently tugged, and the knot swelled, then gave way. Now, quickly, I hooked my fingers through the loosened loops and began to disentangle.

"What's her name?" asked Harriet.

"Zelda," I said, "and she'd eat you up for breakfast, she's got that much spit in her." *My fierce bad Rabbit.* I smiled at the thought of her. The knot melted. The ties fell, straight and smooth, each to its side. My fingers tingled with that feeling they get whenever they've done a job and done it right: ripped out a crooked seam or straightened a bent wire or wiped up a messy spill.

"Thanks," said Harriet. "Thanks so much." She pulled on both sides of her cloak so that it settled evenly across her shoulders. "You're good at this. I'm betting Zelda gets her ties in knots all the time."

How nice that sounded! Harriet saying Zelda's name like that! Just the way you would say, "It's a fine day" or "I live on the next block over." As simple as a greeting. As commonplace as a sunrise. I soaked up the sound.

"Oh, you don't know! Hair ribbons lost, hems falling down, shoes full of holes. Always her face covered in *schmutz*," I said. "Once, she tied my bootlaces in such a knot . . ." But I didn't finish that story.

"She keeps you busy," said Harriet, smiling pleasantly. She tied a neat bow under her chin. "Thanks for saving me from myself," she said, pointing at the bow.

"Oh, sure," I said, wanting to keep her there. I would have stood talking with her for hours— about hats and Zelda and shopkeeping and anything else. It was a joy to just talk with someone. Not like with Freyda and all her craziness and big, sad eyes. Not like with Mama and the constant fighting.

But Harriet started to walk away, to head west down Washington Place toward the park. She was done.

"Can I ask you?" I said, trying to come up with a question that would hold her. "How old are you?"

Harriet stopped and looked at me oddly, and a thin shade fell over her face so that I knew she was about to tell me a lie. "Twenty-one. Why do you ask?" Her voice was a little chilly.

"I thought you were younger, that's all," I said. She was so small, so baby-round, so helpless when it came to tying cloaks and threading machines. I had thought she was closer to my age. *Why would she lie about that?* I wondered. She wasn't underage. That's the only reason I could think of that a young girl would lie about her age.

"How old are *you*?" she asked.

"Sixteen," I said. "I went into the Triangle on the day after my sixteenth birthday."

Harriet raised her eyebrows. "Oh. I thought you were older."

"I'm tall," I said. "People always think I'm older."

Harriet shook her head. "It's not just that," she said. "Well, good night." She turned and began to leave again.

"I'm walking that way," I said, starting toward her and pointing down Washington Place. Maybe I would go to the park before hunting for feathers and trimmings. Zelda loved Washington Park. "Where do you live?"

Harriet stopped and turned to me. "That's personal," she said.

"Really?" I'd never thought of that. On the East Side, your street was practically part of your name. I couldn't have told you how many times I'd introduced myself as "Essie Rosenfeld from Orchard Street." It's just how people did.

"It is," said Harriet, and now she'd gone all stiff on me. "Why would you ask where I live?" She seemed angry, like I'd pulled up her skirts in public.

I took a step back. "It's just a question people ask," I said. "I didn't mean nothing by it. Why are you mad?"

"I'm not mad," she said. "What a thing to say. I don't *get* mad. But I think that's an odd question to ask, and I'd rather not answer it."

I raised my hands to show her I meant no harm. "Suit yourself. Like I said, I didn't mean nothing." All the warmth was gone from the evening. "Have a good night."

She hesitated. I had the feeling she couldn't quite decide whether to walk off in a huff or apologize. "You, too," she said at last. "And thank you again. And . . . and . . . I'll see you tomorrow at work."

"Right. Tomorrow."

Then she hurried off down Washington Place, and I waited a respectful time to follow, but it turns out I waited too long, because when I got to the park, I couldn't find Harriet at all. She'd disappeared in the gloaming.

Huh, I thought to myself. All of a sudden, it was as if all the blood drained out of me, seeping out of my shoes and into the grass. I was so tired, more tired than I could ever remember being in my whole life. I sank down onto a bench and thought, *I can't take another step.*

I watched the people as they hurried home from work or out to their evening engagements and thought about the new girl. *I wonder where she lives?* I looked at the white marble arch that seemed to glow at the north end of the park. It was built by that rich man, that famous architect who got killed that night, all those nights ago, and I remembered reading about it in the papers while I sat with Zelda on my lap, playing our game.

Oh, it's you.

It didn't seem so long ago. I looked around the park, and couldn't help feeling that Zelda was hiding right here, ready to pop out and surprise me.

Here, then gone.

Disappeared in the gloaming.

Killed in an instant.

It was all so muddled, my thinking.

I wanted to get away from it, away from the thoughts that circled my head. I stood up. I would begin again to look for the things I needed to finish Zelda's hat. Determined to find at least the silk for the frame.

And also, one day, to find out where Harriet lived.

Harriet — The New Girl — Mystery Woman.

March 10, 1909

I've gone to bed because of my monthly. Mama frowns. She doesn't approve of this. She says the best thing is to ignore the pain. "Ignore the whole thing," is what she told me the first time, when I was thirteen.

But this I can't ignore. Hot fists have taken hold of my insides and are twisting, twisting until I feel like I can't even take in a breath. A weight, like a cannonball, is pressing on my stomach. My guts have gone loose and I worry that I won't make it to the toilet the next time I have to go.

I roll over onto my side and try to curl away from the pain, try to protect myself from it, like it's something outside of me trying to find its way in. Two knives, heated over coals, are plunged into my back. Every move I make sinks them in deeper.

Even though I know the pain will pass—in a few hours, in a day at most—I think to myself, *Let me die. Please, God, let me die.*

At least Mama let me stay in bed. She gave me a clean rag and took the bloody ones to soak and spread a torn blanket under me, warning, "Don't get any on the sheets." I hear her in the kitchen doing the ironing that I should have finished. The clank of the irons against the iron stand makes me think of prisoners in chains.

This pain is a dark tunnel, and I am afraid of it.

Zelda walks in and puts her head next to mine. "You sick, Essie?"

I don't lift my head from the pillow. "Sort of." I

don't want her to know. I don't want her to know that this is what she's got to look forward to.

"You gonna die?" She asks this very simply, like she might ask if I'm going to finish the pickle on my plate.

"No," I say. *But I wish.*

"Read to me," she says. She pushes a book into my hands.

"Zelda, I don't feel like it," I say, but she doesn't hear me. She's climbing up on the bed and thinking about the book—not about me.

So I open the book, and she crawls into the curve of my body.

This is a fierce bad Rabbit; look at his savage whiskers,
and his claws, and his turned-up tail.

This is Zelda's favorite book. I gave it to her on fourth birthday. It's the only book she owns. I don't like the story much, especially the messy ending, but Zelda loves it. She asks me to read it to her again and again, every night before she goes to sleep. I don't even need to look at the words. I've memorized every page.

This is a nice gentle Rabbit. His mother
has given him a carrot.

Zelda stares intently at each picture as if she could bring it to life. Her face is so close to the book, I can feel her moist breath on my fingers. She is lying against my stomach, which is awful for me, but I don't say anything because I'm worried she'll move and make it worse. I'm trying to keep both of us as still as possible. Her sharp elbows dig into my *kishkes* every time she shifts her weight to point at the pictures.

> *The bad Rabbit would like some carrot. He doesn't say, "Please." He takes it!*

Zelda cheers. She loves it when the fierce, bad Rabbit takes the carrot.

"*Sha*, Zelda. Don't jiggle the bed like that," I say. "You're making it worse for me." Zelda twists herself around and kisses the curve of my waist very gently. But when she turns back to the book, her elbow accidentally knocks into my mouth and I bite down on my own tongue.

"*Oy!* Crazy one! Stop!" My tongue is bleeding. I am like something slaughtered, bleeding all over.

She's pointing at the page, her voice rising in excitement. "Read!"

Here comes the part of the book Zelda loves best. The man with a gun comes and shoots the tail and whiskers right off the fierce, bad Rabbit. *Why?* I think to myself. *Why shouldn't the fierce bad Rabbit want some carrot? What makes the good Rabbit so good that he deserves all the food? And where is the mama of the fierce, bad Rabbit? Why isn't she taking care of her baby?*

But Zelda isn't thinking about any of this. She

claps her hands loudly when I shout, "BANG!" and jumps up when the fierce, bad Rabbit runs by without any tail or whiskers.

"I am a fierce, bad Rabbit," she shouts, hopping on the floor on all fours.

"No," I say. "You are a good little bunny. A kind and gentle bunny." But I know it isn't true. She *is* a fierce, bad Rabbit, and I love her so. Sometimes I think this love I have for her is so ferocious, it will eat me alive.

Mama walks in with a hot water bottle in her hands. She scowls when she sees Zelda running about the bed. "What are you doing?" she says to me, laying the bottle on my stomach and turning me over onto my back. "You're supposed to be making her quiet for bed. Instead you are working her into hysterics! Zelda, come lie down."

"I am a fierce, bad Rabbit!" Zelda shouts again, and leaps at Mama as though she will scratch her apron to shreds.

"That book!" says Mama. "A waste of money. I should have said no when you begged the dime."

Zelda is trying to use her pretend claws to climb up Mama's skirt, but Mama will have none of it. "Zelda, stop!" She swats at her. "Come in the kitchen and I will make for you some sugar milk to settle your brain." Zelda runs into the kitchen. Before Mama leaves the bedroom, she says, "Enough with that book. I don't want you reading it to her no more. It makes her like something wild."

Mama walks out of the bedroom, and I am left alone.

I close my eyes and think to myself, *If I died, who would take care of my fierce, bad Rabbit? Who would love her the way I do?* A wave of pain rolls over me and through me. I turn my head and moan into my pillow, snapping my teeth together as if I could bite the pain in two. As it flows away, emptying me out like the water in a harbor at low tide, I think to myself, *How unfair, to not even be allowed to die.*

I fall asleep with the taste of blood in my mouth.

Chapter 4

"WHY YOU COME HERE AND NEVER BUY?" ASKED the old Chinaman behind the counter.

I shrugged my shoulders as I fingered a bolt of *mousseline de soie*. It had a gorgeous hand. "Nothing worth buying," I said, dropping the fabric.

"Go on, then! Go on!" he scolded, shooing me out the door. We both knew I would be back the next night, and maybe that night the old man would make a sale.

I walked east on Canal. It was only eight o'clock. Mama was probably still awake in the flat. The last thing I wanted was to go home to face her. I decided to walk to the library. The library would be bright and full of people. The library would be open late. I could stay late until after midnight, reading the newspapers for free or browsing the shelves for new books. There might be something for Zelda. A new bunny book or maybe a rhyming alphabet.

It was when I crossed Allen Street—busy, noisy Allen Street—that I started to feel like something was following me. I turned to look over my shoulder, but no one behind me seemed to notice me at all. Still, I couldn't shake the feeling, and I looked back again and again as I walked.

By the time I got to Essex Street, I was nearly running, pulling my shawl tight with one hand and holding onto my hat with the other. I couldn't have said what I was running from, but every bone in my body was shouting *find shelter*.

Just before crossing the street, I looked south toward the river and saw a knot of boys hanging out in an alley. Right off I recognized some of Saulie's gang: Ernie Schowalter, Benny Fenton, and that tough little Italian kid who ran with them. There were others, too, about ten in all, but I didn't know most of the kids Saulie hooligan'd with these days. They weren't from the neighborhood, and he sure never brought them home. But if he kept on running with that pack, he was going to end up in The Tombs for sure.

The Tombs was the big jail on Centre Street. It's where every East Side crook, big or small, landed. Kids like Saulie got sent up for nicking coal or setting ash cans on fire. As far as I could see, Saulie was writing himself a one-way ticket. I'd been saying that ever since Papa died.

I couldn't see Saulie in the crowd, but I knew he'd keep me safe, so I hurried over. They were all staring up at the sky like they expected money to drop. *What kind of craziness is this?* I wondered.

"Ernie Schowalter," I said. "What are you doing here? What's up there?"

"Heya, Essie," said Ernie, but Benny Fenton started to back away when he saw me. "Your crazy brother, that's what's up there. He's gonna jump across the alley!"

"Wha'd'ya mean?" I asked. "He can't do that. Where is he?"

"On the roof! *Yah*, see." Ernie pointed up, but in the black of the night, I couldn't see anything. "He took a bet. If he wins, we each of us owe him a quarter."

Then a voice fell from the sky.

"Hey, I made it to the roof! I'm up here. Can you see me?" A few pebbles hailed down on us. Ernie caught one in his mouth and had to spit it out.

"Watch it, would'ja?" he shouted. "I'm eatin' rocks down here."

Then Saulie's head appeared, sticking out over the edge of the roof of one of the buildings that ran along the alley. It looked like his head wasn't attached to anything. Like it was just a floating balloon against the black night sky.

"Saulie, you get down here," I shouted.

The alley was a narrow one, just eight feet wide, but the roof was four stories up. If Saulie fell, he'd be breakfast for the crows.

"What? Essie? Is that you?" Saulie called down, leaning farther over the edge and giving me near a heart attack. "Aw, shit and feathers! What're you doin' here?"

"Saul Rosenfeld, you get down here. I mean it. You come down here now!" I screamed. I didn't care who heard me. I could see the whole thing. All of it. I could see Saulie running, his foot slipping on the pebbles, trying to stop at the last minute but not being able to and then pitching over the side and falling. Falling. And the smack, the terrible smack of his head hitting the pavement. The eggshell sound of his skull cracking open.

I could see it all, and again I looked over my shoulder because I had the feeling that something was creeping up on me. Something dark I couldn't name.

"Aw, Essie, go home," shouted Saulie. "You're spoiling all the fun."

"Don't you talk to me about fun! You should be home right now, Saulie. Home with Mama."

"Yeah, well so shouldn't you. So don't go telling me what to do."

The head disappeared. The boys in the alley started to whisper.

Is he really gonna . . . ?

Holy shit, mister, I think he's gonna do it . . . .

He better not land on me . . . .

I felt the whole world tilt to the east, tilt as if it were sliding, the buildings shifting, the roofs rising and falling, so that the jump was eight feet across and straight uphill.

"Saulie Rosenfeld, I'm callin' the cops. Right now, I am!" I shouted.

As soon as I said "cops," the Italian kid took off. Benny Fenton had already inched his way to the street, and he started to run, too. Then they all took off, like cockroaches when the lights come on. Even Ernie, who hung on the longest, gave me an ugly stare, then spit and took off.

So, I was alone when Saulie jumped.

He looked like a bird, his arms outstretched, the white of his untucked shirt billowing behind him. A bird against the black sky with nothing but air beneath him. Halfway across, his cap flew off his head. I saw it floating like a seagull wheeling over the garbage down by the docks.

I held my breath. I heard the crash. The skidding of pebbles as he landed on the roof. The bump and bang as he rolled over.

His cap landed at my feet with a soft *whump*.

And then his voice shouting, "Hey, I did it! Did you see me? I did it! Pay up, ya ugly mugs. Every one of ya's!"

By the time he climbed down, dropping the last ten feet from the bottom rung on the fire escape, I had picked up his cap. The blood that had frozen in my veins was starting to run again, and Saulie had crowned himself king of the world.

"Hey! Where is everybody?" he asked, surprised by the emptiness of the alley.

"They ran away because I said I'd call the cops." I stuck out his cap. With a look that said *I oughta kill ya*, he grabbed it from me.

"Did they see me, though? Did they see me jump?" he asked, jamming the cap back on his head. He was half a foot taller than me. Two years younger and already taller. The man of the family now. The man of the family, jumping off of roofs.

"They didn't see. They ran before you jumped."

"Are you shittin' me?" He ripped his cap off his head and slapped it on his leg. "They didn't see? Aw, c'mon! They won't pay if they didn't see. Christ on a crutch, Essie, you ruined everything."

I slapped him then, good and hard, right across the back of his stupid head. "Don't you *never* . . .

never again. If you'd slipped, if you'd missed . . ."

"Aw, Essie, quit being such a spoilsport. If *ifs* and *buts* were soups and nuts, we'd all be eatin' like kings. I *didn't* slip. I *didn't* miss. I made it. Like I was a bird. Like I was a goddamn bird up there!" He pointed to the sky, and I think he really believed he could fly.

Who knows, maybe he could.

All I know is I'd almost lost him. Lost him for good. And even if he was a dope and a hooligan and a junior thug-in-the-making, he was still my brother, and I couldn't bear it if I lost him. I just couldn't bear it.

He shook his head again and let out a loud sigh, staring up at the sky like he was remembering what it was like to fly. Then he stuck out his bony elbow for me to hook through, and I did. We walked a little ways, and he stopped all of a sudden and asked, "Did I show you this one yet?" He took a quarter out of his pocket. I was about to ask, "Where the hell did you get a quarter?" when I decided to bite my tongue and not ask. He placed it in the palm of his hand, then he waved his hand and the quarter disappeared. With a big show, he reached into his own mouth—his own mouth!— and pulled the quarter out.

"Not bad, huh?" he said.

"Saulie, you're something," I said. "I don't know what, but you're something."

"I'm gonna add it to my act. Wha'd'ya think? Good, huh?"

Saulie wants to be the next Harry Houdini.

LOST

Everybody—everybody—has dreams of getting off the East Side.

We walked home, arm in arm, not saying much to each other, but me liking now the quiet emptiness of the street.

And the dark thing—whatever it was—hung back, in fear of my brother who could fly.

September 16, 1909

I am sitting on the fire escape wrapped in a blanket
with Zelda on my lap. The day was warm, but now
the light is fading and the September air is turning
cool. Zelda cuddles in closer, a warm burrowing
animal finding her way back into earth. If I'm
lucky, she'll fall asleep, giving me the chance to finish my library book before the light is gone.

The window next to ours opens, and Jimmy
sticks his head out. "Hey, Essie," he says, climbing
onto his fire escape. Zelda, the fierce, bad Rabbit,
shoots up out of her burrow.

"Hey Jimmy!" she calls. "Come over here!"

"Okey-dokey!" he says.

"Don't!" I shout, but it's too late. He is making
the leap from one fire escape to the other. The gap
is about five feet. If he did it the slow way, he could
stretch his long legs, scissor-like, from one to the
other, carefully putting his foot where the bar is
missing on ours, and I could bear to watch. But he
never does it that way. He jumps and catches hold
of our railing, trusting to God that his foot will land
right where the space is. Every time he does this, I
feel my heart stop beating. I can see him falling,
imagine him tumbling through air, all the way to
the sidewalk below. It must be the worst feeling in
the world, I think, to fall through air like that and
then smash.

Zelda is all squirmy and giggles now that
Jimmy is here. I'm feeling a little squirmy myself.
I'm fourteen, just old enough to be thinking about

boys in a general way. But Jimmy, he's a man, twenty years old, and studying to be a lawyer. I shouldn't be thinking on him at all.

Zelda climbs onto Jimmy's lap and strokes his nose, running her finger over the big bump on the bridge. Jimmy lights a cigarette. Mrs. Pelz doesn't allow smoking in her flat.

"Is that the Napoleon book?" asks Jimmy, helping Zelda get all her limbs tucked up.

"No, I returned that one yesterday," I say.

"Aw, the devil! I wanted to read that when you were done." He blows the smoke from his cigarette into a high plume over Zelda's head. It looks like the curling gray feather for an imaginary hat on her head.

"So check it out yourself," I say.

"I should, but I never will." He shrugs his shoulders. "I'm too lazy! I count on you to do the legwork, you know. If it weren't for you, I'd be a complete imbecile."

"A *lawyer* imbecile," I point out.

"The worst kind! God save us from lawyers!" he says. More than once, Jimmy's hinted that it's his parents' idea, becoming a lawyer and all. His parents live in Yonkers and own two shoe stores and part of a paper mill. They have big dreams for their only son.

"Jimmy, will you do cat's cradle with me? Huh, will you?" Zelda is bouncing impatiently on his lap. I wish she would settle down and be quiet. I don't get so many chances to talk with Jimmy about the books I'm reading.

"Hush, Zelda," I say. "Jimmy doesn't want to play cat's cradle."

"Sure I do," says Jimmy. "Go find your string and bring it back out here." Zelda scoots in through the window and Jimmy winks at me. "There's more than one way to skin a cat," he says. He moves closer to me and says, "Hey, it's getting colder. Share some blanket, will ya, Ess?"

"Get your own!" I say. It's fun to joke with Jimmy. He's always got the right spirit.

"Okay," he says. "I'll get my own," and he stands to cross back over to his fire escape.

"No!" I shout, grabbing onto the leg of his trousers. "I'll share. I'll share. Just don't jump!" He settles back down, smiling. "You big oaf!" I say, passing him half the blanket. We make a tent between our legs, our toes pointing at each other's.

"So what's that about?" he says, pointing to the book and taking a long drag on his cigarette.

"It's about the world," I say, looking at the thin gray book in my hands. "About the whole world, and how it's made up of nothing but particles. Little specks so small you can't even see 'em. You and me and this fire escape and that building and even the air and the water and the planets and stars—all of it—it's all made up of little particles."

Jimmy nods, like he's heard this before, but doesn't say anything, just waits for me to go on. The next part is hard to put into words. I haven't finished the book, so I'm not sure I've got it right. "And everything's falling apart, all the time," I say. "That's the important thing. Everything. Even while we're sitting here talking. This building is slowly crumbling, and this metal"—I rest my hand on the fire escape that holds us in air—"is turning to rust. And all the people are slowly dying. Even civilizations are creeping to their ends, and the stars, every one of 'em, are burning out. All of it— it all falls apart."

Jimmy looks at me. He's sitting with his elbow dug into his knee, his chin in his hand, the burning cigarette held close to his face. The cigarette sends up a screen of smoke between us. "What do you make of that, Essie?"

I like the way he asks me that—what I think. Most grownups don't. Mama never does. Mrs. Pelz never does. My teachers at school never did, when I used to go to school. They didn't want to know what I *thought*. They just wanted to know what I *knew*. There's a big difference.

But Jimmy says I have original ideas. So even though I'm just fourteen, and he's six whole years older than me, we talk about all kinds of stuff. And he really *is* lucky that I go to the library every week; else he wouldn't know a thing.

I look out over the railing of the fire escape, through open air and up to the sky which is dissolving into an inky puddle.

"I think that I *should* think it's sad and upsetting, everything going to pieces like that. But I think—" I stop because I'm not sure how to put this into words. I've been thinking it in my head but haven't said it out loud to anyone. Things always sound different deep inside my own brain, where there's quiet and harmony and open arms. But then when I say them out loud, there's somebody there to shout, "That isn't right! What a stupid idea!" and sometimes my thoughts come out all wrong and not what I meant to say at all. Mama says I spend too much time reading all those books what she thinks are rubbish. Sometimes Zelda and me, we sneak off to the library, and then tell Mama the shopping took extra long.

"I think," I try again, "that what the book doesn't say is that out of all that destruction, something new is born. You know how when a tree rots to the ground, it makes something else grow. Or like how when someone dies, we give that name to a new baby. Something new comes from out of the death."

"Cat's cradle!" shouts Zelda, sticking her fist with a ratty piece of yarn out the window. She climbs onto the fire escape and faces Jimmy with a pout. "It's broken, though!" The yarn has come undone, its limp and raveled ends hanging from her clenched hand.

"Come here," I say. "I can fix that." I take the unraveled ends and wind them together, then stick the whole thing under my tongue so it's soaked in spit. I rub the join back and forth between the palms of my hands 'til I can feel the yarn get hot. I check it for strength. It holds. The ends have felted together, a seamless loop. You can't even tell there was a break.

Jimmy stubs out his cigarette and gives Zelda his full attention. It's funny to see his thick, stupid, man-hands try to make a Jacob's ladder. Zelda tells him to "Sharpen up!" a few times. While they play, I dive my nose into the book, catching the last of the dying light.

If I could freeze the world in a single moment, this would be it. A good book, Zelda laughing, and Jimmy close enough to touch. It's everything I want. Sometimes, I pretend that we're a family. Jimmy's the papa, and I'm the mama, and Zelda is our little girl.

Life should be like this, I think, sitting on the fire escape. Without any holes, without any heartache. Everything holding together. Forever.

Chapter 5

Saturday evening, and Washington Park was alive. I sat on a bench and watched the parade of people go by. Couples strolled, arm in arm, on their way to a restaurant or show. Dark-suited businessmen in homburg hats hurried to get home in time for dinner. A few kids played kick the wickey by the fountain, while two or three others tossed jackstones on the pavement.

As I watched the sun settle into its cradle in the west sky, I felt my heart sink. A heaviness draped itself across my shoulders. I thought I would never move again. It was the end of the work week. Tomorrow, a day off. The first warm day of spring. The trees frothed with budding leaves and the air felt like a mother's warm embrace. Why was I crying?

I was tired, that was all.

I looked in the faces of the people passing by, wondering if they knew what I knew about this park. It was once a potter's field where they buried poor people and bums. Twenty thousand people were buried here. Did they know? That elegant couple there, the gentleman wearing a silk top hat, the lady in her fur-trimmed coat—did they know they were walking on the bones of twenty thousand people, buried without ceremony, buried without anyone to weep by their graves, buried without a stone to hold their names?

The unknown dead. Forever peeled away from their names.

And then, across the fountain, there was Harriet, walking home from the Triangle, her small, velvet purse hanging at her side. She walked slowly, with her coat unbuttoned, and when she got to the fountain she stopped and took her coat off and hung it over her arm.

The sight of her filled me with such a desire, and I wanted to run up to her and throw my arms around her and say, *Take me away from here, please.* She was stopping to straighten her hat. She was resetting the pin, threading it in and out of the black straw boater she wore.

I stood up and crossed the path, but then I stopped. I remembered how angry Harriet had gotten when I asked where she lived. My desire suddenly shifted, and more than anything else I wanted to know where Harriet Abbott lived.

I decided to follow her.

I knew she didn't want me following her, but I did it anyway. Sometimes, even now, I think of all the things that would have gone differently if I hadn't followed her that day.

She was easy to follow, she moved so slow, like a barge on the East River. But that's how she spotted *me*. When she crossed out of the park and headed for the market on West Fourth, I was just twenty feet behind her and didn't realize how close I was until she caught sight of me in the reflection of the candle shop on the corner.

"Are you following me?" she asked, turning around so quickly her skirt bloomed like a primrose around her feet.

What I should have done is this: I should have gone all stiff and angry and shouted, "Of course I'm not! Do you think you own the streets of New York?" Instead, I stood there with my mouth hanging open and the look of a half-wit on my face, until she asked, very sharply, "Why are you following me?"

I closed my mouth and pulled myself up straight. *Go down with dignity*, isn't that what they say? "I wanted to see where you lived, is all. You made such a big deal out of it the other day, I got curious. That's all." I shrugged my shoulders. "And I'm sorry. I guess it was rude of me. It *was* rude. So I'm sorry."

She looked around then, across the street and back at the park and behind her, too, like she thought there might be someone else following her besides just me.

"I'm a private person." She said this like it caused her pain.

"I'll say," I answered, under my breath.

"What does *that* mean?" she asked, irritated.

I shrugged again. "It means you've been in the shop for a whole week and hardly said two words to anybody. You're the quietest person I ever met."

"I've always been quiet," she said, then looked down at the coat draped over her arm. "Dull, I suppose."

I reached across and took her hand and gave it

a little squeeze. "You don't seem dull to me," I said. "Look, would I have followed someone who's dull? You're the Mystery Woman!" I waved my hands as if clouds of stage smoke engulfed her.

Harriet laughed, and it was a nice laugh—a little on the quiet side, but still nice.

"You want we should get something to eat at the market?" I asked. "Or," I pointed at her gloved hand, "I suppose you're going home to your husband?"

She fanned out her hand as if she could see the ring right through the glove. "No, my husband isn't home tonight."

"So," I said, shrugging my shoulders. "We could cook up something quick, like maybe a stew with vegetables—or a soup if you got the broth already?"

She stiffened a little. "You mean at my apartment?"

I shrugged again. "Sure. How bad can it be?"

She turned her head slightly and looked over my shoulder, and I could tell she was having a whole conversation in her head that she didn't want me to hear. I wondered then if maybe the husband *was* home, and if maybe she was a little afraid of him. Some girls have to worry about their husbands' tempers. Some girls can't bring friends home. I tried to make it easy for her.

"We could just get a roll and some coffee," I said, pointing up the street to the market. "We could sit in the park."

She shook her head. "I'm tired." Then she

straightened up a little. "Yes. Let's buy a few things at the market and go back to my apartment. That's the best idea. It will be nice to have a guest. I haven't entertained in forever."

It turned out Harriet's apartment wasn't bad at all, and it was right across the street on Washington Square South. The building was a little dumpy, but at least there were gas jets on the stairs and carpeting in the hallway, even if it was ripped in a few places.

"It's actually a good thing that it's torn," said Harriet, pointing to a spot in the corner near her door that was peeling away from the floor. "That's where I hide my spare key." She rummaged a little in her purse and then pulled a key out, holding it up like she'd just pulled a diamond out of a pile of horseshit. "A small miracle! I managed not to lose it today." She opened the door, and we went in.

From the hallway, we walked straight into the parlor. At one end of the room, three large windows, floor to ceiling, let in the last of the fading light. There was a fireplace, cold and unlit, and a sofa with a low table in front of it piled with books. But what really caught my eye was a scarred and scratched-up piano—one of those baby grand kinds—stuck in the corner.

"A piano!" I said. "Look at that!"

"It's a piece of junk," said Harriet, taking off her hat in front of the mirror over the fireplace. "It came with the place. All of the furniture did."

"A piano!" was all I could say. I rested my hands on the black wooden top of it, then let just one finger press down a key. It made a sad sound that hung in the air like a bird so high in the sky you can't tell it's moving at all. I didn't know a single person who owned such a thing. "Zelda's always wanting one of these. Always, she's begging me for a piano."

"She wants to learn how to play?" asked Harriet, coming over to stand next to me.

"No, she wants *me* to learn how. She wants me to play the piano so *she* can sing and dance. Zelda's got ideas for going on the stage someday."

"Really?" said Harriet, a curl of disapproval in her voice. "That would be quite the life."

"Mama won't even hear of it," I said. "She says they're all no-goodniks and worse what run around on the stage. But Zelda, she's got her mind all made up. She's gonna be a star. Bigger than big."

"Well, bring her around, then," said Harriet. "I know some of the new songs." She sat down on the low bench and launched right into "I Wonder Who's Kissing Her Now." We sang all the words together, straight through—her voice thin and weak, and mine all off-key, and we nearly laughed our heads right off our necks when we finished.

"What else can you play?" I asked.

"Lots, if I could see the music," said Harriet, squinting in the fading light. "Here." She handed me a box of matches. "Would you mind lighting the lamps? I hate striking matches. It always sets my nerves on edge." So I lit the two gas jets on the wall and the kerosene lamp on the piano. Harriet shuffled through the sheet music on the piano rack and

played "In the Good Old Summertime," and then
"Let Me Call You Sweetheart" and "Steamboat
Bill." We sang everything, and we were just awful,
and honestly I couldn't remember when I'd had
that much fun. And all because of a piano. Zelda
was right! We should get one!

"I'm hungry," said Harriet after we tried
singing the harmonies for "Down By the Old Mill
Stream," and agreed we had to give up on that one.

"*Oy*, we should'a started the stew before
singing," I said. "Where's the kitchen?"

Harriet showed me where and then sat down at
the kitchen table and folded her hands.

"You could help, maybe, a little?" I said, raising
one eyebrow at her as I shoveled the ashes out of
the stove.

"Of course," she said. "What should I do?"

"Chop the onions. Or the carrots. I don't care
which." I finished cleaning out the firebox and
grate and had just set the coal for lighting when I
saw that Harriet was staring at the onion like she
didn't know which end was up.

"Don't tell me you've never chopped an onion,"
I said.

She shook her head sadly. "I really haven't.
And I have no idea how to begin. What do you do
with this rooty part?" She pointed with the tip of
her knife.

"You're the living end, Harriet!" I said, taking
the knife away from her. The last thing I needed
was her chopping her own fingers off. "How do
you feed your husband?"

LOST

"My husband's dead," she said.

The knife hung in the air, pointing at her. It felt all wrong like that, so I put it down on the kitchen table, and I said, "I'm sorry. I didn't know."

I thought back to how she looked that first time she walked into the shop—how I thought she had lost something, and she said it was her key. But now I knew it was something more. And I thought how just a few minutes ago she'd looked at her ring finger and said that her husband wasn't home. What had it cost her to say that simple truth?

It's a terrible thing to lose someone you love.

I heard about a man once who jumped off the Brooklyn Bridge because his wife had died, and when he hit the water, it ripped the clothes right off him. The police fished his body out of the East River, and he was completely naked.

Grief is like that. You smash up against it, and it rips all the outer parts of you away. You're left naked in front of everybody.

I turned my eyes away, looking down, and picked up the knife and began to chop the carrots with careful, gentle strokes. "Were you married long?"

"Six months." Her voice was flat. "He died in that explosion on the New Jersey pier. The one in February. He had business in Jersey City that day, and he was on the ferry when it happened."

I remembered that day. Everybody did. It was a work day. I'd just stood up from my sewing machine. It was the noon break and I stood up and suddenly the whole building trembled and my chair seemed to slide away from me an inch or two. Then I heard glass breaking far off, and the sound of fire engine bells ringing in the streets. But there was nothing else after that, and so—*eh*, we had our lunch. What else could we do? The world is always coming to an end somewhere.

But Harriet, what had she thought? I wondered. Waiting, maybe alone in her apartment. Had she heard by then that there'd been an explosion on a New Jersey pier? Did she know her husband had business that day across the river? Did she sit in the dark, waiting for her husband to come home and light the lamps?

How could she bear that?

There was a long silence as I tried to think of a thing to say, the right thing to say to someone who has lost everything like that, but the only words that came into my mind sounded stupid and untrue. All those things that people say when someone dies—*God has a plan; Time will heal the pain; You'll meet again in heaven*—those words are weak and pathetic, and they just made me feel angry, bitterly angry, so I didn't say anything at all.

"I'd rather not talk about it," said Harriet. "It was a shock when it happened. I'm much better now."

I nodded. I understood not wanting to talk about certain things. If anything like that happened to me, I wouldn't want to talk about it, either. "Is that why you came to the Triangle?" I asked. "Because you have to take care of yourself now?"

Harriet nodded. "The money's all gone." She

shrugged. "I don't know where it went. I thought it would last forever, but it's all gone."

She stood up and brought down two bowls and two cups from the cupboard and placed them on the table in place settings. I pushed the sliced carrots to the edge of the table. The fire would be hot enough soon, and if I stuck to it, we could be eating within the hour. It was the least I could do.

Before I sliced into the onion, I stuck five matches in my mouth, the way Mama taught me to do. The matches stuck out from my pressed lips like spokes on a wheel.

"What are you doing?" asked Harriet.

I couldn't talk with the matches in my mouth, so I scooped them out. "It makes it so your eyes don't water. Because of the onion," I said, then stuck the matches in my mouth again.

She was the one who started with the laughing, and you know how it is after you've been in one of those awful, sad situations and then you laugh? How the laughter just rips itself out of you and tears right through your chest? That's how we laughed, God forgive us. That's how we laughed. We laughed 'til we cried, and the tears—I don't know if it was from the onion or the laughing— rolled down both our faces.

Nu, in the end we had bread and cheese and coffee for supper, and it was just as good as the stew would have been. We sang some more songs at the piano, and we talked some about the books she had—mostly novels, which I wouldn't give a crooked penny for—and then we settled on the sofa and she said, "It's getting late. Won't your family worry after you?"

"Nah," I said, looking at the clock over the mantle and thinking how wonderful it was to *sit*, just to sit. It seemed like this was the first time in two weeks I had stopped moving. "Mama goes to bed early on account of she works in a bakery. She don't wait up for me most nights. She knows I can take care of myself."

"What about Zelda?" asked Harriet.

"My little *Zeldaleh* is asleep by now," I said. "I'll have to sneak in so I don't wake her."

We were quiet for a minute, and then I asked, "What about *your* family? Can't you go back to them?"

Harriet shook her head. "My parents disapproved of my marriage. They won't let me back in the house."

"What about brothers or sisters? Don't you have any?"

"One sister, younger than me. All she thinks about is her coming-out party and who she's going to marry. And I have a younger brother, but we've never been close. And then, I have my older brother. John." She paused. "We used to be very close. Best of friends, really."

"So why not write him a letter? Or go see him? He'd help you out, wouldn't he?" I couldn't imagine Saulie turning his back on me if I needed help. *Never* he would do that.

Harriet was holding a round, silk pillow on her lap. In the center of the pillow, there was a tufted tassel, and she ran her fingers through it over and over again. "I've wanted to, so many times. My writing table is filled with letters I've written to John, but never mailed. You just don't understand, Essie. You don't know the trouble I've gotten myself into."

Money trouble. Maybe she'd borrowed too much? Maybe her husband had been a gambler? Or a drinker? There were so many ways to sink yourself into debt, and once you were there it was like trying to claw your way out of a cellar pit.

Harriet changed the subject, asking me more about Zelda, and we talked for another hour. When I was sure that Mama would be in bed and asleep, I said it was time to go.

"I enjoyed this," said Harriet, as we said good-bye at the door. "I hope you'll come again." Then she stretched up on her toes and gave me a quick kiss on the cheek.

Out on the sidewalk, as I passed by her building, she rattled open the window and stuck her head out. "Next time, bring Zelda! We'll dance!"

I waved at her and shouted back, "I will!" then headed home through the dark and empty streets.

October 5, 1909

Zelda and me are waiting at the fountain. Jimmy is going to meet us here at noon, as soon as he's done with his morning classes. I look down Washington Place, knowing that's the way he'll be coming. His law school building is the one right next to the Triangle Waist Company. Freyda's older sister works there, and Freyda is going to start working there this summer, soon as she turns sixteen, and I'll probably get a job there, too, when I'm old enough.

I make myself turn away from Washington Place and begin to count to sixty. Here's how the game goes: If I don't look for a whole minute, then Jimmy will appear. And when he does, I'll look surprised and say, "Is it noon already? I didn't even notice the time!" That way he'll see that I wasn't all anxious and eager for him.

Zelda's running circles around the fountain. I don't know where she gets the energy from. It's too cold to wade in, but she's dragging her hands through the water and already I can see she's got her sleeves wet up to her elbows. The ribbon I tied in her hair this morning has come undone. It's hanging on by a single loose knot.

"*Zeldaleh*, come here," I say. "Your ribbon, I gotta fix." She won't stop, though. She's like a train on a track, chugging and chugging, and nothing can stop her.

I turn back to look up the street. No Jimmy yet. I let my mind wander, imagining what it might be like, me working right next door to where Jimmy does his studying. I wonder if sometimes we'll meet for a cup of coffee at the noon break. Or if he'll walk me home, the way fellas sometimes do with the factory girls. I've seen them meeting up after work on the sidewalk under the streetlamp. The fellas bring a penny bag of candy, or sometimes a nosegay, and then they offer up their arms, and the two of them walk off. Freyda says her sister has been walked home by lots of fellas, but she hasn't brought even one of them up to meet her mama and papa.

Zelda is swinging with another little girl. They've grabbed hands and are going 'round and 'round like a crazy carousel. At first, the little girl is laughing just like Zelda, but then I can tell she wants to stop. She yells out, "Quit it! I don't want no more," but Zelda doesn't hear. She keeps swinging and laughing.

"Zelda, stop!" I say. "Enough with the swinging. She don't want." I wave my arm to bring her in. When Zelda finally lets go, the girl goes flying back and lands on her *tuches*, crying and holding up her scraped hands for her mama to see.

Oy vey! There's shouting then, and lots of crying, and the mother is shaking her finger at me and saying that Zelda is *wild* and oughta be locked up somewhere, and I'm giving her back a piece of my mind with interest, when all of a sudden Jimmy is there and offering everyone penny licks from the ice cream pushcart and the tears dry up just like that and everything's quiet again.

So we finish up our ice cream and give our glasses back to the vendor, and then we start to walk down East Fourth, Zelda holding Jimmy's hand, and me with my two hands just hanging down at my sides, all empty and a little surprised to be so. Zelda's chattering on and on about the organ grinder who came down our street this morning with his funny monkey in a red cap. Zelda loves to give a penny to the monkey, just so he'll tip his cap at her before grabbing the coin.

Jimmy's wearing his out-and-about clothes: brown sack suit, white collar that Mrs. Pelz starched to a military stiffness, a brown bowtie, and a homburg on his head. I feel proud walking next to him, even if he's paying all his attention to Zelda. He's such a fine-looking gentleman, and I think everybody must know it just by looking at him. The sun is shining to beat the band, and a cool October breeze is blowing just enough so I don't need to worry about sweating through my blouse, but not so much that I'm worried about my hat blowing away. It's a new one I just finished trimming yesterday, and already I've got two girls in the neighborhood asking me to make one just like it for them.

We turn down Broadway and then we're at Zelda's favorite shop — Mitchell's, where they sell pianos and other musical things. In the window, there're three pianos — a shiny black one, a walnut brown one, and a gleaming white grand that looks like it's whipped out of the same ice cream I just ate. Zelda puts both hands up to the glass and presses her nose right up to it. She'll leave snotty marks, I know, and I hope the storekeepers don't come out and yell at us.

"Can we go in?" asks Zelda.

"Better not," I say, thinking of her grubby hands on all that polished wood.

"Aw, why not, Ess?" says Jimmy. "I bet they get folks coming in all the time who aren't gonna buy. Why not us?"

So we go in, and Zelda's pointing at the ones she likes best and making a cartload of noise, but no one seems to mind that we're there, so Jimmy and I walk behind Zelda and look at all the beautiful pianos. Some of them are new and some are used and some play all by themselves by turning a music roll that plucks out a song. Zelda likes these ones best.

"Can we get one, Essie?" she asks, her voice hushed.

I'd laugh, except I know it would hurt her feelings, so I just say, "No, honey. We can't." The pianos cost eight hundred dollars, more money than Mama makes in two years.

"They're so beautiful," she whispers and starts to sway in time to "Shine On, Harvest Moon."

Jimmy smiles at her and says, "You should be on the stage, Zelda." Then he turns to me and says, "Her and you, both."

"Me?" I say, shocked at the idea of it. "Not me!"

"Why not you? You're pretty enough to beat out any chorus girl for a spot."

"Jimmy Eagan, you are such a liar!" I say, my face turning the color of a boiled beet.

"No, sir, I'm not," he says, leaning against one of the uprights and taking a long look at me. "I went to a show last Saturday, and the chorus girls all looked like lumps of mud. You could'a out-shined 'em all."

"Oh, go on!" I say, and now I'm determined to prove him wrong. "I can't sing, for one thing, and I can't dance, for another," I say.

"Aw, singing and dancing, that's not what fellers go to the show for."

I've heard that I'm a "looker," but never really believed it. Mama only once *ever* said I was pretty, and that was when she told me I didn't need to bother to learn the good cooking because I had a face what would fool a man into marrying me. Then she added in a dark voice, "You make sure those looks don't get you into trouble."

At home, there are no mirrors. Mama took them down after Papa died and never put them up again. Am I pretty? How would I know? Reflected in a shop window, my face looks watery and thin to me.

"Listen to me, Miss Essie Rosenfeld," Jimmy says, taking both my hands and looking right into my eyes. "You're one of the prettiest girls I ever met. Mark my words, in a few more years you'll be breaking hearts in a line all the way from here to Philadelphia. And if I was a few years younger and you were a few years older, why I'd be at the front of that line, you'd better believe it." Then he gives both my hands a good squeeze and drops them, just as he turns to look at Zelda who's got a crowd around her at the front of the store.

A player piano is playing "Wait 'til the Sun Shines, Nellie," and Zelda is singing the song in her strong, clear voice that never hits a wrong note. She's waltzing in a circle, holding her skirts out around her, dipping and twirling at just the right moments. She's only four, but there's so much bravery in her, so much joy and life, that people can't help but stop and watch her. When she finishes, everyone in the store claps, and I hear one of the clerks say, "That kid oughta be on Broadway."

It's hard to get Zelda out of the store after that, because she's eating up the attention faster than she gobbled up her ice cream. We cut across Bleecker and then down Allen, and pretty soon we're in our own neighborhood with the sounds and smells and sights we know best: housewives haggling with peddlers over a bucket of fish, pickles in barrels, the flapping and fussing of chickens in crates waiting to have their necks wrung. No fancy piano shops here. But plenty of ladies' corsets, shoelaces, and eggbeaters—sold right on the street for your convenience.

"Couldn't we, Essie?" Zelda is still harping on the piano. "If'n you saved up *all* your hat money, couldn't we get one?"

"No, Zelda, not if I saved up all my hat money for a century!" She's pulling on Jimmy's hand like a goat on a short tether—until she sees a friend on a stoop tossing beanbags, and then she runs off to play with her.

"You know," says Jimmy, "I saw a sign in the store. They sell those things on the installment plan. Not so much each week, if you can come up with the down payment. You don't think we could maybe scrape together enough—"

"Don't you even think on it, Jimmy Eagan!" I say. "I can see it now! Saulie in The Tombs for pinching coal, and the rest of us in the poorhouse for not paying the rent. Oh! But at least Zelda will have her player piano, God forbid she should ever suffer!" But the whole time I'm saying this, my heart is swelling and I'm thinking, *Oh, good-heart Jimmy! Jimmy what loves us like we're family!* And I can't help but imagine what kind of a husband he'll be for the lucky girl that catches his heart for her own.

Chapter 6

"OH, WE MISSED THE PARADE, DIDN'T WE?" SAID
Harriet. She was standing in the parlor, looking out
the window. I was sitting at the piano, plucking out
"In the Good Old Summertime." Harriet had
taught me the song bit by bit each night, and now
I had the whole thing learned. Imagine that! In one
week, *me* playing a whole song at the piano. It
sounded slow and plunky, but at least you could
tell what it was.

I stood up and looked out the window to see
what she was talking about. On the street corner
were three musicians—one playing a fiddle, another
a flute, and the third had a penny whistle. People
were clapping in time to the music, and one man had
broken out in an Irish jig.

"Oh," I said, going back to the piano. "The
Saint Patrick's Day parade." Well, why pretend I
was interested? There's never been much love lost
between the Irish and the Jews. To tell the truth, I
wouldn't bother to turn my head to see a whole pla-
toon of them parade up Fifth Avenue.

"Have you ever taken Zelda?" asked Harriet.

I made a sound halfway between a pig snorting
and a donkey braying. "No sir! Drag ourselves
forty blocks up town to see a bunch of Paddies in
top hats and green sashes? No thanks."

"She would like it! It's lively! Promise you'll

take her next year," insisted Harriet.

"Yeah, sure I will," I said, waving her words away. It wasn't worth my breath to argue. I sat back down at the piano and played the opening notes of my song. "When did *you* ever see the parade?" I asked. "What? You came up all the way from Philadelphia for it?" Harriet had told me her family was from Philadelphia.

Harriet plucked at her hair, rearranging the wispy curls that fell about her face. "Once or twice. We were in the city already," was all she said. Then she picked out a book from the bookcase and sat down on the couch to read.

Harriet's books didn't interest me, but I left the piano to sit next to her anyway. Her books were all novels or awful poetry. The one she had in her hand right now was a collection of stories about girls who were engaged to be married — simpering, droopy girls with names like Cecilia and Lucilla who gazed into moonlit gardens and wondered about the nature of love. I wished she had something with history in it, or science.

"You don't have anything good to read," I complained, stretching my legs out on the low table in front of the sofa.

"*That* is ridiculous," she said without even looking up.

"Show me one good book," I said. I was really just trying to irritate her so she'd give up reading and talk instead. I liked talking with Harriet. She was good at making conversation.

"Oh, where to even begin?" she said, putting

down her book with a big show. She stood up and went to the bookcase. "Here's Mrs. Wharton's newest collection." She tossed a book onto my lap. "And then here is *The Gate*, translated from the Japanese. And here's the latest from Wodehouse, and—"

"But none of it's real," I said. "It's all just make-believe."

"It's better than real," she said, giving a firm nod of her head. "It's true."

"That doesn't make sense," I said, but I thought maybe I *did* know what she meant. Sometimes you can know all kinds of things about a person—their name, and where they were born, and what they do for a job—but you still don't *know* that person. Not in an important way. Facts are not the same as truth.

"Listen to this," she said, pulling another book down from the shelf. When she opened it, I could see the book was called *Howards End*, which of course made me think of someone named Howard who had a large rear end.

"Stop laughing," said Harriet, with the same look my fourth-grade teacher used to give me just before I stopped going to school at all. But I couldn't. At least not until she started reading. Her voice was trembling and she held onto the book with both her hands, as if it were the last lifeboat lowered from a sinking ship.

Only connect! That was the whole of her sermon. Only connect the prose and the passion and both will be exalted, and human love will be seen at its height. Live in fragments no longer.

That was all she read, but to her I could see it was the whole world held in those words. They didn't mean anything to me, those words, strung together like paper lanterns across a deserted back alley. But they meant something to Harriet. They were her one small truth wrapped up in something unreal.

So I didn't laugh. I didn't say anything.

"To write like that," she finally said. "To write just one thing like that. I could die then, and be happy."

"So," I said. "You should write."

"I've tried." She shook her head slowly. "Oh, believe me. Horrible stuff. I'm embarrassed to even think of it now."

"You wrote—like that? A novel?" I asked. It seemed extraordinary to me that someone could actually do that—write a novel. I'd never known anyone who wrote a whole book.

"Short stories," she said. "And some poetry. I sent two of my stories to *McClure's*, but they were both rejected. Well, like I said, they were horrible."

"I bet they weren't so bad," I said.

"Yes, they really were," she answered. "I could prove the point—they're stuffed in my writing desk over there—but I'd die of shame if you ever laid eyes on them."

Harriet stood up and put the book back in the bookcase, then she walked over to the window and looked out over the park. "Did you know Edith Wharton used to live just over there? On Washington Square North, number seven." She pointed to the east end of the park. "Henry James was born on Washington Place." Then she pointed west. "Willa Cather lives over there now. At number eighty-two. I walk by her house almost every day. One of the geniuses of our age."

"Is that why you and your husband moved here?" I asked. "Because of all the writers?"

Harriet was still staring out the window, her face turned away from mine. "I wanted to live here for years. I begged my father to let me get an apartment in the Village. But he said it was out of the question. Inappropriate. He said people would talk. I daresay he was right. People do like to gossip."

"Unmarried? A girl living alone?" I said, shaking my head. "I never heard of such a thing." Some of the girls in the shop, the ones who came to America without families, lived in boarding houses, but that wasn't the same as living alone. The mother in the house always watched over those girls, telling them when they could come and go, keeping a sharp eye out. Sometimes those mothers even wrote to the girl's family back in the Old Country.

"Is it really such a scandal?" asked Harriet, bitterness in her voice. "A woman living alone—independently. Thinking her own thoughts. Doing as she pleases. Living a life that's unfragmented."

"I just never heard of such a thing, is all," I said. On the East Side, a girl lived with her parents until she got married. Even a widow, like Harriet, usually moved back home. Living without family; it didn't make any sense to me. It was nothing I wanted. It was the *last* thing I wanted. "So, is it what you hoped it would be? Living with all the writers around you?"

Harriet left the window and went to sit at the piano. She played the opening bars of a sad song, one of those *Etudes* by Chopin that she played for me sometimes. The song was like smoke in the air. It filled the room with a thickness that made it hard to breathe.

"It turns out my father was right," she said, at last. "He told me, 'A good writer can write anywhere.' And I'm not a good writer. So there it is. Just one more disappointment in life."

I went over and put my arms around her. "Don't cry, Harriet," I said. She leaned over the keys, her small shoulders rising and falling beneath my arms, and I wanted somehow to usher her into a safe harbor. She seemed so alone. She seemed so lost. "You'll write your great book someday. I know it. Look. Don't cry. Do you want a pickle? I have one in my bag."

Harriet choked and then laughed. "A pickle?" she said, looking at me with tear-clouded eyes. "My life's dream is lost and you offer me a pickle?" And then she laughed some more and said, "Yes, actually. I would love a pickle." So I went to my string bag and pulled out the newspaper-wrapped pickle left over from lunch and gave it to Harriet. The crumpled piece of newspaper, I was about to throw it in the fire when I noticed a headline in small letters: LOST. *Isn't that funny?* I thought. *I was just thinking that word*—lost—*and here it is in the paper.* I wondered what the article was about, so I folded up the page and put it in my pocket, saving it for later.

"I don't know what is the matter with me these days," said Harriet, crunching so loudly on the pickle that it made *my* mouth water. "I cry at the drop of a hat. I never used to be like that. I *never* used to cry. Even as a child."

"Well, it's no surprise," I said, sitting on the couch and picking up the books that Harriet had taken down. "You just lost your husband. Anyone would cry after that."

"Yes," said Harriet, pausing mid-bite. "That makes sense." She finished the pickle, and I didn't say what I was thinking or what I was pretty sure *she* was thinking, which is that there wasn't one thing in the flat, *not one thing*, that showed a man had ever been there. No stray suit coat in the wardrobe, no shoes by the bed, no tiepin or shaving brush or cast-aside hat. No photographs. No watch chain. No paper cuffs.

And even if you could convince yourself that Harriet had removed every trace of her dead husband—so painful was the memory, she couldn't bear to live with his things—there was something else missing. Not once in all the hours of talking did she ever tell me even one story of her husband. Not once.

I looked down at the book I held in my hands, the newest collection of stories by Mrs. Wharton.

It was called *Tales of Men and Ghosts*. I slid the book back into its place in the bookcase. *That's right,* I thought. *Men leave behind stories of themselves.* But in this flat there was nothing but an eerie, echoey silence around Harriet's lost husband. A silence too quiet even for a ghost.

March 9, 1910

I'm scrubbing the kitchen floor. I have rags tied around my hands to keep them from bleeding. Without the rags, the sand grinds into my palms, turning them to hamburg. This is a trick I learned from Mrs. Pelz, who has scrubbed a floor or two in her day.

I finish the last corner of the floor, the one under the slop sink. It's the worst part. There's mold there, where the puddle collects. The pipe is rusted and flakes of iron are sprinkled like sugar on an apple cake. Scraps of old food, dried and hardened, stick to the floor.

Now I must sweep and sweep, catching every last grain of sand with my broom before I spread the borax and water. The sand has done the hard work of scouring away the grit. The borax will kill the germs and make the room smell fresh.

Zelda's out the window, sitting on the fire escape. I've made her promise to sit far away from the end with the missing bar, and she's being a good girl. I have all the windows and the front door open to draw a breeze into the flat. It helps to dry the floor faster. She's dropping paper parachutes onto people's heads, ones she made out of pieces of old newspaper.

She just turned five, and I won't let her go out in the street by herself. Zelda squawks about this. She wants to go play with her friends, but I won't bend.

"*Nu*, when you're six," I tell her. "Then you can

go out alone, but only as far as our block, no farther! When you're six. Now be a good girl and tell me what you see, while I'm finishing the floor."

She sits on the fire escape, holding a penny in her hand. I've promised her she can spend the penny in the street when I'm done with the floor.

She tells me every detail: "Essie, the fish peddler, such fat ones today! Look only how big!" "Here comes the policeman with his stick. Ooh, he gonna get those boys!" "Mrs. Bornstein! Hiya, Mrs. Bornstein!" "There he is! The banana man! The banana man!" She reports every peddler, every argument, every pigeon that poops on the street below.

I finish rinsing the borax, hoping I didn't use too much water this time. Last month, Mrs. Horowitz who lives below complained that her ceiling leaked after I washed the floor. Is that my fault, I ask? Still, I don't need neighbor trouble, so I keep my mop close to dry.

I go into the bedroom to strip the sheets so I can air them out over the fire escape. I need to check one of the mattresses, the one that Saulie sleeps on. During the day we keep the mattresses piled on the bed, but at night Saulie pulls one into the parlor.

Sure enough, there's a tear in one corner of the mattress. I wouldn't wonder if Saulie did it with his knife to hide something from Mama. A deck of cards, or one of those magic tricks he buys at that shop, or even a cigarette. He's twelve already and going to hell in a handcart.

I feel around in the mattress, which is stuffed with straw and feathers, but can't find anything there that shouldn't be. I fold the mattress in two and hoist it onto my head. Then I take it into the parlor. In the parlor, I notice the blanket box against the wall, and I decide I'll air out the blankets, too. Everything will be good and fresh today.

But when I pass the blankets out onto the fire escape, Zelda isn't there. I stick my head out, just to be sure. I hear music floating up from the street—the plinky, uneven notes of a hurdy-gurdy. But no Zelda. What kind of disappearing act is this?

"Zellie?" I call as I walk through the rooms—through the kitchen, into the bedroom. She's not there.

I walk back into the kitchen and look around. The only piece of furniture I haven't moved out of the room is the dish cupboard, so I look in there, even though I know Zelda can't fit.

Oy, now she's playing the hide-and-seek?

It's when I'm closing the door of the cupboard, turning the little scrap of wood that serves for a latch, that I notice the open front door. I look out into the hallway. I knock on Mrs. Pelz's door, knowing she's out doing the marketing. Her door is locked.

I lean over the railing and look down the dark stairwell. "Zelda?" I call. I begin to walk downstairs, and then I break into a run. By the time I reach the street, my head is on wheels.

I look one way on the street, toward Broome,

and then the other, to Delancey. In every direction, there is the press of people and pushcarts and horses, and so much noise it makes my ears crack.

I need to run, but I have no idea where. Delancey is the busiest street on the East Side. If Zelda has made it that far, she will be run over by a horse and wagon, I am sure of it.

"Mrs. Klein, have you seen Zelda?"

"*Neyn*, Essie."

"Mrs. Zuckerman? Zelda, have you seen?" I am asking every person I know, but no one has seen her. She is so small. How could they have noticed her in all this mishmash?

"*Kindele!* What can it be?" asks Mrs. Pelz. She is suddenly at my side, her market basket over her arm.

"I have lost Zelda!" I shout. "She's on the street, but I don't know where."

Mrs. Pelz grabs my shoulders and gives me a shake. "Only to calm yourself!" she says. "We will find, we will find." A horse and carriage clatter past. We stare at it, thinking the same thought. Mrs. Pelz points up the street. "You go that," she says. "I go this," and she hurries toward Broome.

I run as if the cops are after me. At the intersection of Delancey, I look left and right. Which way to go? I can't think. I can't choose. I stamp my foot. *I have lost her.*

All around me, peddlers shout out the song of the streets.

Herring! Pickled! Herring! Chopped! Firm and fresh herring!

Livers and tongues. Livers and tongues!

What's life without onions? I have the sweetest on the East Side!

And floating above and around the shouting and bargaining, the music of the hurdy-gurdy.

Zelda is nowhere.

I feel like a giant hole is opening up inside of me.

The music from the hurdy-gurdy plays on, and I follow the sound. Left on Delancey. There is the organ grinder in his wretched jacket, his greasy bowler hat. There is his little monkey, running up and down the grinder's arm, depositing coins into the man's pocket.

And, of course, there is Zelda, waiting her turn to hand her penny to the monkey so that he will tip his small red cap to her.

I walk slowly toward Zelda so I don't frighten her with a rush. She doesn't see me, she's staring so hard at the little wrinkly monkey with the long, curled tail.

It's her turn. She stands in the middle of Delancey. So serious, she leans in from the waist and holds out her penny. Just as serious, the monkey snatches it from her hand and tips his cap.

Zelda squeals with delight, then catches sight of me. She is so happy to see me! She points at the monkey and crows.

"Oh, it's you!" I say, as if this is just a game. As if we have been playing all day, and here is the happy end of it.

Later, Mrs. Pelz will tell me to take away

Zelda's supper. Mama will tell me to lock her in the bedroom for the rest of the day. She must be punished, they will both insist. But these things, I can't do.

At this moment I am so happy to have her back that all I can do is catch her up in my arms and whisper, "Come here, my fierce, bad Rabbit," then kiss her on her nose where her whiskers used to be.

Chapter 7

"GOOD! WE'LL HAVE IT ON SUNDAY, THEN," SAID Harriet, looking happier than I'd seen her for days. "I *love* tea parties. They're my favorite kind of party to organize. Especially when they're just for the girls." She was lying down on the couch in the parlor with her bare feet up over the arm. Her ankles had been swelling up at work the last few days, and the first thing she did when she got home was take off her lace-ups and prop up her feet.

"I can't quite see it," I said, squinting at her. "You, a social hostess." I was sitting in the straight chair, slicing apples into a bowl. My plan was to cook them up with some cabbage and carrots and make a sweet stew. I'd been craving sweetness all day.

"Eldest daughter. It was my job," she said sourly. "Does Zelda like tea? She doesn't drink coffee yet, does she?"

"Zelda drinks everything. And eats everything. Don't plan the menu around her," I said.

"I'll set the table by the window. I'll get flowers. And those little cakes with the sugared icing that they sell in the bakery on West Fourth."

"Harriet, please! You know what those cost? You can't afford," I said, shaking my head. There was a happy buzzing in my brain as I imagined Zelda here in Harriet's apartment. I could see her

97

running first to the piano and then to the table set with a white lace tablecloth and flowered teacups. She would ask a million questions. Harriet would finally hear her sing. We would all dance! Under my breath, I started to hum.

There was only a shadow of something at the very edge of my dreaming that felt heavy and a little anxious. That same dark and nameless thing that haunted me from time to time.

"You're forgetting," Harriet said. "Sunday comes *after* Saturday, and Saturday is payday. Don't tell me I can't afford to buy three little iced cakes for a party!"

"I'm just saying. It's near the end of the month. Rent's due in a week. Nobody buys cakes at the end of the month." I was cutting the apples paper-thin so they'd cook fast. Both of us were hungry. Mrs. Gullo had kept us late because of the busy time of year. Everybody buys new waists in the spring.

"Well, then that's the smartest thing I've ever done," said Harriet. "Because I paid a full year's rent when I let the apartment."

"You what? That's crazy!" I slipped the last apple slice into my mouth and picked up one of the carrots. I could turn carrots into coins in half a minute. "How'd you have the money all at once?"

"I just did," Harriet said, staring up at the ceiling. "It didn't seem like so much at the time. I figured, take care of it all at once. Who needs a landlord coming around every month knocking on the door? So I paid the whole year up front."

LOST

"You and your husband?" I asked, looking at her, the carrot held still in my hand. I never said her husband's name out loud. Gerald Abbott. Neither did Harriet. There was something about the actual name that sat heavy on my tongue.

"Yes. My husband and I." Harriet closed her eyes and seemed to drift off somewhere.

Once the fruit and vegetables were in the pot and simmering, there wasn't much to do until they were cooked through. Harriet had gone into her bedroom and was trying to find something "appropriate" to wear to the tea party. I went back to the parlor and practiced my song—my one and only.

"Don't dress up for us," I shouted so she could hear me. "We'll be wearing our everyday clothes, you know." In truth, Zelda would probably want to put on one of her special dresses. I breathed a mighty sigh of relief: Thank God I hadn't let Mama throw them out when she complained about how much space they took up.

"Of course!" Harriet shouted back. "No need for you. Come as you are. But I'm the hostess! I should look presentable, at least. This old thing I wear . . ." Her voice trailed off, and I heard her digging deep at the bottom of the wardrobe.

I looked at the sheet music on the rack in front of me. *How does anyone make sense of it?* I wondered. Lines and dots jumping up and down on the fence rails that ran across the page. Some of the dots were open, some were closed. The lines were either joined or all by themselves, and some of them waved little flags from their tops. It was ridiculous!

Impossible! And yet Harriet would look at these scribblings and play the most remarkable music.

I shuffled the pages and looked at the names of the composers. *Those*, at least, I could read and make sense of. Handel. Haydn. Beethoven. Brahms. Most of them had been dead for years. Mozart, I knew, had been in his grave for ages. But Harriet could bring him back to life, all because of those lines and dots and squiggles. It was like Mozart could speak from beyond the grave.

I played a few of my memorized notes—*In the good old summertime, in the good old summertime*—and wondered if the dead really did talk to us in some way. I'd heard the stories. Whistling teapots and flying tables. Pictures falling off the wall. A voice in a dark room. Smoke signals from a bowl. People earned their living in this trade—gypsies and fakirs. But maybe the dead really did speak to us— in other ways.

"This will do," said Harriet, walking into the room holding a lightweight woolen dress in a soft gray. "It isn't—" She looked at the dress with a critical eye. "Well. In another life, I would have said this dress was impossibly wrong. But in another life, I had fifty dresses in my closet, and now I have four, so this one will do."

"It's beautiful, Harriet," I said, fingering the skirt. The fabric was finely woven and the seams stitched so small and tight you couldn't even see them. The skirt draped from the waist like a water-fall. It was simple, with just two rows of jet-black buttons up the front for decoration. Sturdy, well made. A little plain, but clearly excellent. "Did your mother buy it for you?"

"No. I bought all new clothes when I came here." She shook the dress vigorously, then hung it up on the arm of the gas jet next to the fireplace so she could look at it. She spotted a loose thread and plucked it off, then smacked the hemline two or three times to shake loose any dust. "I didn't take one thing from my parents' house when I left. I even sold the clothes I walked out in."

I stood up next to her and looked at the dress, imagining the hat I would pair with it if I could. Something in straw, but edged with a silk band for finish. And lilac trimmings to lighten the gray of the dress — flowers in silk and velvet. I could see it all inside my head. My fingers felt that familiar tingle, ready to set to work on a new hat.

But then I thought of Zelda's Merry Widow, the one I still hadn't finished. Lately, I'd been spending all my time after work at Harriet's. I still hadn't found the black organdy, the drooping ostrich feathers, the silk ribbon. All I had was the frame made of wire, a ghostly skeleton of what could be. Zelda was probably furious with me. After all, I had promised it for her birthday. Guilty, I tried to push that thought out of my head. Tomorrow, for sure, I would find the organdy.

"You're *that* mad at them?" I asked Harriet. I didn't like to think of a family ripped apart like that. I had an urge to stitch them back together.

Harriet slipped her arm around my waist and rested her head sideways on my shoulder. "It's really more about them being mad at me," she said, still looking at the dress. "And yes. I *am* that mad."

"I thought you didn't get mad?" I said.

"Surprise!" said Harriet, and I could tell by the crack in her voice that *she* was the one who was surprised. "Now, here's the problem," she said, dropping me and stepping forward. "I can't fit into the darn thing. Ever since you started cooking supper every night, I've put on weight. Have you noticed?"

"*Eh*, maybe a little. On you, it looks good."

"Good or not, I can't squeeze myself into this dress. Do you think I could let out half of the tucks without ruining the look?"

I shrugged. "You could try. And even if it looks bad, you could make a sash to cover it up. Something darker, in a silk, maybe? You could make that, easy."

"You have the best ideas, Essie," she said as she carried the dress into the bedroom.

I left the parlor to check on the stewing vegetables. While I was stirring the pot, Harriet called out, "I want to send out a proper invitation. To Zelda, I mean."

"*Oy, gevalt*, Harriet, she's just a little kid," I said, tasting the stew and burning my tongue. *Damn.* "You don't need with the invitations and the cakes and everything *zhuzhed* up like we're the Astors and the Vanderbilts."

"No, I want to. I want her to see what a real invitation to a tea is like," she shouted. "I want it to be special. You know, I was always very good at organizing parties. All my friends said so. Of course, I was a complete failure at attending them, but at organizing them, I was a champion."

"Dinner's almost ready," I said. "Maybe ten more minutes." I sprinkled a little salt and pepper into the pot, and then added a generous tablespoon of sugar.

"Essie, can you look in my writing desk? I think I still have some lavender-scented notepaper. Would you look for me?"

I stuck my head in the bedroom. Harriet was sitting on the edge of her bed, leaning into the circle of light thrown by the kerosene lamp and ripping out the waistband of the gray dress. "You don't need with the special paper," I said.

"Please go look!" she said, not even raising her eyes from her work.

I went to the writing desk in the parlor. The folding desktop was closed, but not locked. I pulled over the little chair Harriet kept against the wall and opened the desktop up. The middle drawer, the one between all the cubbies, was locked, but everything else was out in plain sight.

I started to look for the stationery.

In the three cubbies on the left, there was nothing lavender-scented: store receipts, newspaper clippings, three horse chestnuts, a map of the city, a few pamphlets. In the cubbies on the right, I found an envelope with some postage stamps in it, a small silk-and-feather bird perched on a tiny nest, a list of New York publishers, a train schedule, a dried maple leaf, and a paper accordion folder.

I took out the folder, untied the string, and opened it. The smell of lavender floated up from the sheets of paper inside. I slid them onto my lap. But instead of blank stationery, I found a pile of letters. Each one was written on a piece of dove-gray paper, thick and gorgeous and scented with lavender. Harriet's peculiar handwriting marched across every page, the *t*'s like church spires, each *y* a trampled snake.

I only read a line or two of each, and stopped reading altogether after the first few. It isn't that I was overcome with some delicate sense of privacy. On the East Side, everybody's nose is in everybody's business, and you just get used to it. That's what it's like to live with too many people in one tenement and toilets on the hall and fire escapes that connect and no locks on anything. The only person I knew with a lock on her bedroom door was Mrs. Pelz, and that was because she'd been taking in boarders for so many years.

No, it wasn't some sense of respect for Harriet's private letters that made me stop. It's that I knew I was holding Harriet's heart in my hands. Looking at those letters, it was like she was lying on an operating table, all opened and pink and bleeding, and I didn't want to risk hurting her in any way.

2 March

Dear, Dear John,

If I could undo what I have done, I would leap to do it, and turn myself once again into your too-serious little sister who spends all of her time with her nose in a book . . . .

7 March
My Dearest, Darling Brother,
Every night I weep to think of the pain that I have brought into your life . . . .

18 March
Dear John,
Can you forgive me?

I closed the folder up. I tied it shut. I put it back in the cubby.

Why was my hand shaking? Why was I frozen in that chair as if I'd turned to stone?

Harriet had *told* me that she wrote to her brother. She'd *told* me that she didn't send the letters, just kept them in a pile, gathering dust. Of course they'd be in her writing desk.

My eyes were stinging. I felt like my belly had dropped down to my boots. I couldn't seem to get up. I kept telling myself, *Move on.* But I didn't. I was stuck.

I just hadn't known . . . I hadn't expected. It was the grief that caught me off guard. The mourning. The sorrow.

"I've ruined it, I think," said Harriet, walking in with the dress in her hands. "What do you think?"

Harriet had ripped the waist seam out so that the skirt hung loose, attached to the bodice by just a few threads that spewed from the gap. The dress looked like a person cut in two, and the threads made me think of what spills out when you gut a fish.

"It looks dead," I said.

"Well, that's a pretty thought," said Harriet. "I'll make a sash. Cover the whole mess up. You didn't find any good notepaper?" I shook my head. "Well, then, I'll go to the stationer's and buy a penny sheet and an envelope, too. Don't even tell me I can't afford it!"

She laid the dress on the sofa, like it needed to rest to recover, then she headed for the kitchen. "I'm going to serve the stew whether it's ready or not. Aren't you hungry? I'm about to eat my left arm."

"Yes!" I said, my voice sounding too loud in my ears. "I'll be right there."

I looked at the desk again and realized I'd put the paper folder back in the wrong cubby. It was moved one over from where it had been. I took it out and quickly shoved it in the next one. When I did, I knocked over the bird and nest, and the bird tumbled off. *Oy, gevalt! Always there's something goes wrong.* I picked up the nest to settle the bird back on it and noticed that there was something metal tucked in the bottom, resting in the soft spot where an egg should have been.

It was a key. A small, plain, iron key—too small for a door.

I knew it belonged to the locked desk drawer, even before I fit the key into the keyhole and turned it. I heard Harriet in the kitchen; she was busy setting the plates for our supper on the table. Outside, the sun had set, and the lamps had come on.

I slid the drawer open. Inside the drawer there was a hatpin and a pair of earrings and a stack of envelopes tied up with a cream-colored ribbon. The hatpin and the earrings were a set. The earrings were the delicate drop kind, thin silver threads holding a brilliant blue stone, like I'd never seen before. The hatpin was twelve inches long and sharp enough to kill a person. On its head was a much larger blue stone set in silver filigree.

The envelope on the top of the tied-up stack was covered in canceled stamps. The stamps were brightly colored, red and green, from Italy. I couldn't read the name or address on the envelope; the ribbon that held the letters together covered it up. There was no return address.

I didn't touch anything. It was bad enough I'd opened the drawer. I closed it and locked it and put the key back in its hiding place. Then I hurried into the kitchen.

During supper, Harriet decided I had a headache because I was so quiet. "Lucky for you, I know all the remedies," she said. "My mother gets headaches every month like clockwork." She turned out all the lights, pulled the curtains closed, wrapped my head and ears in a scarf, and made me breathe steam. "It eases the blood congestion in the brain," she said, but all it did was make me sweat around my hairline.

"I think I'll go home," I said when Harriet finished clearing the dishes. "I could use a lie-down."

"That's the best thing of all," said Harriet. She wanted to give me money for a cab ride, but when she looked in her purse, she realized she didn't have enough. "Ridiculous," she muttered. "A ridiculous way to live. Not having carfare. Thank God payday is just around the corner."

"There's plenty of leftover stew for tomorrow," I said. "I won't be able to come over. I have some errands I need to do."

Harriet frowned. "I guess I shouldn't expect you every night!" she said. "I've gotten used to it, though."

"Me, too," I said, giving her a quick kiss on the top of her head. "I'll see you tomorrow at work."

"Work," she muttered again. "A ridiculous way to live."

That made me laugh. I don't know how anyone could call Harriet dull. Quiet, yes, but never dull.

July 15, 1910

I am sitting at the kitchen table staring at the Dover eggbeater I just bought. I turn the crank and watch the twin beaters go around, perfect little dancing partners who never crash into each other.

Zelda is under the kitchen table, and she is pouting for two reasons. The first is that I took the eggbeater away from her. She thinks the eggbeater is a toy, the best she's ever had. If she had her way, she would sit under the table twirling the blades 'til her dying day. "Zelda, give already," I said to her. "I've got work to do with that."

I am going to make an *omelet*.

This is reason number two why Zelda is pouting. She doesn't like eggs. As if she knows what she likes! Not even six years old! Such an expert on eggs she is, she can say that she won't eat a nice omelet?

"I won't," she says from under the table. "Eggs stink worse than doo." She's singing a song she made up called "The Stinkin' Egg." She sticks her head out from under the table and says, "You can't make me."

Like I can't!

I'm ignoring Zelda. Mrs. Farmer says that children should eat at least one egg a day. It's a perfect food, she says, and will keep away all kinds of sickness.

It was a bad spring. Ever since Zelda went out into the street to give her penny to the monkey, she's been sick with one thing or another. Fevers through March, a cough all through April. And then in June, she got dysentery and lost her color. It's July now, hot and sticky, and I'm afraid of typhoid taking hold of her because she's weak and has never gotten her blood back.

I've decided I'm going to feed Zelda an egg a day, whether she likes it or not. Where I'll get the money for that, I don't know, but I've made up my mind.

I have Mrs. Farmer's *Food and Cookery for the Sick and Convalescent* checked out from the library. It's open on the table in front of me. I am looking at page 114, and already I don't know what's what. Mrs. Farmer tells me I must separate the yolk from the white, but I have no idea how to do this. I crack the egg into a bowl and carefully scoop the yolk out with a wooden spoon. Just as I have the slippery yellow ball near the edge of the bowl, it breaks and all the insides ooze over the spoon, back into the slosh of the white.

It's ruined. I've barely begun and my omelet is destroyed. *Oy!* I throw the wooden spoon into the slop sink.

I have three pennies in my pocket, all that is left of the two dollars I earned making a hat for Mrs. Gurwitz. It was a wedding gift for her niece, and I made it with bunches of silk forget-me-nots and a large *chou* of *mousseline de soie* matching the color of the flowers, stitched on at one side. Mrs. Gurwitz said, "Essie, honey, you've got a calling."

I gave the two dollars to Mama because we were short on the June rent after all the medicines we'd got for Zelda, and she said, "Here, keep back a little," and shoved a quarter in my hand. But after the eggbeater and the ruined egg and the ice cream cone I bought for Zelda, I have just three pennies left.

I hand the eggbeater to Zelda and tell her to stay put under the table. Out in the street, I spot Mr. Kramer right away, but his eggs are never fresh. They have a funny smell and are cloudy.

I walk farther down the street and find Mrs. Weissman. Her cart is fitted with metal boxes and she keeps her eggs on ice. No one in the neighborhood has ever had a bad egg from Mrs. Weissman. That's why she can charge the extra penny. I choose my egg and ask her how to separate the yolk from the white. In Yiddish, she tells me to hold the egg over a bowl and crack the shell in half with a knife. I should then pull the two halves apart, but without letting the yolk slip out. Then I should pass the yolk back and forth between the shells until the yolk is dry. "It's a trick," says Mrs. Weissman with a wink, and takes some practice. But I don't have money to practice. This is my last egg.

At home, I do like Mrs. Weissman said. My hands tremble, but it works, *Gott sei dank*! The yolk is safely in one bowl, the egg white in the shell. I reach under the table and take the eggbeater from Zelda. She screams like a fishwife, but I tell her to put a sock in it.

I plunge the eggbeater into the egg white and begin to turn the handle. The white is supposed to turn "stiff and dry," says Mrs. Farmer, but nothing seems to happen. I turn the handle faster. The egg-beater twists over in my hands and buckles up. Am I doing something wrong? Did I buy a broken beater?

I continue to turn the handle, faster and faster. My left hand cramps up. My cranking arm feels like it will twist itself off. Zelda has crawled onto the table to watch.

"That egg hates you," says Zelda. "It's mad at you for beating it so hard."

"*Zzztt*, Zelda," I say, sweat pouring down me, my hair sticking to my forehead and the back of my neck.

She hangs her legs over the edge of the table and continues to sing her song:

An egg is worse,
Than any curse.
Eat one a day,
You'll need a nurse!

Oh!
The stinkin' egg,
The rotten egg,
The no-good stinkin' rotten egg!

If I hadn't already heard the song twenty times, if I didn't have sweat covering my body like the sludge in the East River, if I weren't busy beating an egg to death—I probably would have laughed at the song. Zelda's good with words and can sing a tune like a bird, but I'm in no mood for cleverness. In the fight between me and the egg, the egg is winning.

I give up after ten minutes. The egg white has bubbles in it and has thickened some. I decide that's close enough to stiff and dry. Mrs. Farmer says:

The success of an omelet of this kind depends upon the amount of air inclosed in the egg and the expansion of that air in cooking.

I'm pretty sure that I haven't "inclosed" enough air, but my arms have turned to bricks. If I keep beating, they will fall off my body.

The next part goes better. I add water to the yolk and beat it until it's thick and lemon-colored. Mrs. Farmer wants me to add one-eighth teaspoon of salt, but I don't have any spoons for the measuring. No one on the East Side does. I throw in a pinch, then one more for good luck.

The last part of mixing the omelet is to fold in the white, and so I wonder, *Why did I have to separate them in the first place?*

Ach! The cooking! When it goes bad, I hate it like pebbles in my shoes.

I put the frying pan on the stove. I don't have an omelet pan, which is what Mrs. Farmer tells me to use, but I hope the frying pan will do. I toss in a *bissel* butter and watch it sizzle and brown in the pan. Then I pour in the omelet mixture and let it set. When the bottom is brown, I take the pan off the stove and put it in the oven to bake. I keep close by, knowing how quickly food can burn in an unwatched oven. The kitchen is one hundred degrees. Mama would kill me to know that I'm burning coal in July to cook one egg.

When it's ready, I take the omelet out of the oven and fold it in half. I'm supposed to serve it with white sauce, but I have no idea what that is, and Mrs. Farmer doesn't explain. I slip the omelet onto a plate and sprinkle a little sugar on top. It looks bare and lonely on the plate all by itself. I think it might be good with some fried onions, or maybe stuffed with some sauerkraut. Something to add a little *zip!* to the tongue. But Mrs. Farmer doesn't give permission for that, so I leave it plain.

"Zelda," I coax, "come and eat your good omelet."

Zelda is in the parlor, singing her egg song and dancing. "Dance with me, Essie!" she says, holding out her arms and swaying.

"Not now, Zelda," I say, frowning.

When she sees the plate in my hand, she twirls away. "I won't!" she sings.

"You will so," I answer. "It's for your health, God forbid anything should happen." I tap the doorjamb three times for luck.

She twirls to the far end of the room as I come at her, and then quickly slips out the open window onto the fire escape.

My patience is all used up. "Zelda!" I bark. "Eat this omelet at once!"

"I'll eat it out here!" she says. "Like a picnic!"

Good, I think. *She gets the sunshine and the fresh air and the egg, all at once.* I hand the plate to her through the window. She is smiling and still dancing her feet to the music she hums inside her head. The plate becomes her dance partner. She dips, she sways, the plate cradled in her arms. Then she flings her arms out, flips both wrists, and dumps the omelet over the side of the fire escape.

My arms reach out. My fingers grasp. I suck in air.

There is no time to watch the omelet fall. There is no sound as it hits the pavement. There is no chance of rescue, no hope for recovery, no time to mourn. In a split instant, it is gone, and all that is left is my anger—blinding, white-hot anger.

"You little *shit*!" I yell.

Zelda's smile slips from her face, like the omelet from the plate. Her eyes show terror, wildness. A frightened sound strangles from her throat. She throws herself to the far end of the fire escape and slips through the missing bar in the railing.

I can see her body tensing up to spring like a rabbit. She is going to jump from our fire escape to Mrs. Pelz's. She has seen Jimmy do it a hundred times. He makes it look easy. She can't possibly understand that there's no way her five-year-old legs will reach. She will fall.

Not one word can I push out of my mouth. Someone has taken a fist and shoved it down my

115

throat and is squeezing both of my lungs. I gasp, a crippled sound, just enough to make her pause.

And now she looks down. Her toes are jammed into the railing, her arms wrapped around the edge, and her body hangs over nothing. Between her and the sidewalk, there is nothing but air. I can see the look in her eyes. She knows. She understands that she could fall. "Essie," she whispers, her voice squeezed through a sieve.

"Don't move," I say. "Only to stay still. I will have you in a minute."

I crawl to the end of the fire escape. Every second feels like a century because in my mind I am seeing her fall. In my mind, she is already falling, she is already gone, and I am on my hands and knees grabbing at nothing but air and the memory of this little girl who was here but is gone.

I reach her and grab a fistful of dress. She folds herself back through the railing. I take her in my arms and hold her close. She cries softly, like an apology, and says, "I told you I don't like egg. I *told* you."

And the thing of it is, she did.

Chapter 8

FOR THE FIRST TIME IN ALMOST TWO WEEKS, I turned left out of the factory and headed toward my own neighborhood instead of Harriet's. It was still light out, though the sun was low in the sky. I could see it hanging over the park as I looked west down Washington Place.

I'd hardly seen Mama in two weeks, and that was all right with me. She left for the bakery before I got up in the morning and went to bed each night before I came home from Harriet's. The few times we'd bumped into each other in the flat, I'd said nothing more than hello. I suppose that was rude. But what was she going to do? Lock me in a room? Lock me up, with no way to get out?

I wasn't afraid of her.

With Freyda it was different, though. She was my oldest friend in the world, and it felt strange the way I'd dropped out of her life. So when she walked up beside me on Mercer Street, my heart gave a little jump and I couldn't help but smile at her.

"Are you going home?" was all she said.

"Not straight off," I said. "I'm going to the library first. You want to come with?"

She shook her head. "I gotta get home."

We walked on a little more and I wondered if she was going to slip her arm through mine, the way she always used to, but she didn't. It felt odd to walk like that, without linking arms. It made the streets feel unfamiliar, like we were walking in some new city that neither one of us knew.

"It seems like you got a new best friend," she said at last. I looked over at her face. Was she angry? She didn't seem so.

"Nah," I said. "I . . . just . . ."

"Don't say anything what isn't true," she said. "Not to me. *Not* to *me*. At least we got that between us, right? We never lied."

I nodded my head. She was right about that. Even as kids, we'd never lied to each other. Like two-bit crooks we lied to our mothers, but never to each other.

"So all's I want to say," said Freyda, "is—" She took a long breath in. She was taking twice as many steps as me, on account of her short legs and mine that were so much longer. It made me remember how, when I walked with her, I had to slow down some. So I did. I started walking half pace.

"All's I want to say," she said again, and now she stopped. Just stopped on the sidewalk and took hold of my wrist. It felt good having Freyda's hand on my arm. I'd been missing it without even knowing. "I understand. I think I do. How it must be easier to be with Harriet. Easier for you. Because there aren't any memories and nothing that's going to make you think—No! Don't walk away from me," she said. I had started to walk on without her, but she tightened her hold on my arm. The craziness in her was coming out again. It broke my heart to think of Freyda being crazy, and I didn't want to see it. "I won't say *anything* about the other," she said. "I'll never say another word about it, if'n you don't want. You have my promise on that. I just want to tell you—that I understand. And if you ever want to be my friend again, I'll want to be yours. No matter what. No matter how long it takes. You're heart of my heart, Essie Rosenfeld, and I'll always love you." She gave my wrist a squeeze and then turned a sharp left onto Houston Street, heading straight into the old neighborhood.

I stood there for another few seconds, watching Freyda's back get smaller and smaller. Part of me wanted to run after her. Part of me wanted to slip my arm through hers. Part of me wanted things to be the way they used to be.

But another part of me whispered *danger*, so I kept going south on Mercer.

Walking up the stone steps of the library made me realize we had books that were due. Zelda and me. The last time I'd been in, I'd checked out *The Tale of Ginger and Pickles* and left it for Zelda on the kitchen table.

Zelda and I went to the library every week, sometimes twice in a week. All the librarians who worked there during the day knew us. Zelda made herself known everywhere she went, and the librarians all loved her. *I'll have to take home a new book*, I thought, *and remember to bring back the other one. She must have read it by now.*

I walked straight up to the large wooden desk

that curved like a balcony. I didn't recognize the librarian sitting behind it, a young woman with her hair neatly pulled back in a loose, low bun at the back of her neck. She was copying something out of a book onto a piece of paper.

"I'll be with you in just one minute," she said, raising a finger, but not looking up from her work. The steel-rimmed glasses on her face looked like they pinched her nose. I imagined her taking them off at the end of the day and rubbing the bridge of her nose in relief.

"Okay," she said, closing the book and looking up with a smile. "How may I help you?"

"Old newspapers, do you have?" I asked. "I want to read about that big explosion, when the dynamite blew up on the pier in New Jersey. But I don't remember the date. Do you?"

"*Hmmm,*" said the librarian, coming out from behind the desk. "That seems like so long ago, doesn't it? I know it was after the New Year. And I know it made the front page, so it shouldn't be hard to find." We walked over to a wooden bookcase, where piles of newspapers were stacked. She handed me an armful. "Why don't you look through these, and I'll start working my way through these."

It only took us about five minutes. When we finally found the paper, we were both surprised to see that it had happened just seven weeks ago. The librarian shook her head and clucked. "It seems like so much longer," she said, stacking the other newspapers in a neat pile. "But that's the way with old news, isn't it? Once it's over, it just fades from your memory."

"Unless you knew someone who got killed," I said, scanning the front-page headline: EXPLODING DYNAMITE KILLS AT LEAST 24; HUNDREDS INJURED, ALL NEW YORK SHAKEN.

"*That's* true," she said. "Did you?"

"Oh, no. I don't think so," I said. She gave me a curious look. I took the newspaper to a table and sat down to read.

The story of the explosion was splattered across half of the front page and all of pages two and three. There were photos of the shattered pier, the deck of the *Ingrid* with its mast snapped in two, a twisted steel boxcar ripped off its track. There were first-person reports from stevedores and roustabouts working at the shipyard who were there when the twenty-five tons of dynamite had exploded.

There was a list of the dead and injured. I scanned quickly for a Gerald Abbott, but there was no mention of anyone with that name. The article said that the exact number of dead would never be known since so many bodies had been blown to bits.

On page 3, I found a small article with the title: FERRYBOAT HIT IN MID-STREAM. The *Somerville* had just left the Jersey slip with hundreds of passengers on board who had taken trains to the dock and were now headed for Manhattan. When the explosion hit, windows shattered, railings splintered to toothpicks, and the boat listed heavily to the starboard side. The horses on board went wild with terror and tried to smash out of their gates. Some people were trampled. But no one was reported dead. Calm had been restored after a few minutes, and the boat had landed, as usual, at the West 22nd Street pier.

I closed the newspaper and wondered. Of course, he could have been on a different ferryboat. Or still waiting on the dock. Or even in the train station, which was flattened. There was so much pandemonium and destruction for miles around. Windows shattered on Ellis Island. People knocked off their feet in the financial district. Fire trucks tearing through the streets of Brooklyn, trying to find an explosion that had happened in another state.

"Did you find what you were looking for?" asked the librarian. She was picking up the books that people had left behind on tables and returning them to the shelves. She stopped and looked at the front-page headline spread out in front of me.

"Not really," I said. But in truth, I didn't know what I'd been looking for to begin with. All I knew for sure was that I *wasn't* surprised that Gerald Abbott wasn't listed among the dead.

"It's an odd feeling, isn't it," she said, "looking back through old newspapers? It always makes me feel out of step."

"Like how?" I asked.

"Well, take for instance the story of the explosion." She nodded her head toward the headline. "It's all anyone talked about for a week. But now, we couldn't even remember when it happened. Or look at that story." She tapped the page, pointing to another headline: SOUGHT MISS ARNOLD LAST THANKSGIVING. "Do you remember that one?"

"No," I said. The name rang a bell, but I couldn't remember why.

"The missing heiress? The one who was walking down Fifth Avenue and disappeared. Right on the street, in broad daylight. Imagine that! A person can just disappear. You *must* remember that!"

Yes, I did. Now that she said that, I *did* remember it. The whole country had gone crazy looking for the girl. Dorothy Arnold was spotted in Chicago. Dorothy Arnold was spotted in Salt Lake City. She was seen in Baltimore and Philadelphia.

But not one of the sightings turned out to be real. Just anxious people seeing what they wanted to see.

"Where did they finally find her?" I asked.

The librarian wrinkled her forehead. "I don't think they ever did," she said slowly. "No. She's still lost. Do you want me to put that paper back for you?"

Lost. That word was stuck in my head. Why? It tickled a part of my brain, but I couldn't figure out why.

Just then I looked up and there was Freyda coming at me like she was being chased by Cossacks on horseback. Her hair was flying out behind her, and her forehead was dripping sweat.

"Essie, you gotta come now," she said, so out of breath she could hardly get the words out.

"What? What is it?" I asked.

"Only you gotta come now," she said, grabbing my arm and pulling. "They got Saulie. He's in The Tombs."

August 23, 1910

We've brought the kitchen chairs into the parlor and made a row of them. Mama is on one end and Mrs. Pelz is next to her and last comes me. It's a steaming hot day in August and I've been cooped up in the kitchen all afternoon while Saulie and Zelda rehearsed in the parlor. They wouldn't let me in, not for nothing. Not even to sit on the fire escape and catch a breeze.

We are waiting for the show to begin.

Today is Saulie's birthday. He's thirteen years old, and this is what he wanted, to perform his newest trick for us. Saulie has dreams of going on the road with his magic act. One of these days, I know, we're going to wake up to find him gone.

For the curtain, Saulie borrowed Zelda's Dressing Room—the two coatracks with the broken broom handle across them—and tossed an old blanket over it. He's wearing a tattered top hat he bought (he *says*) and twirling a wooden cane that belongs to Ira Fishbein's *zaideh*. For added effect, he's chalked a black mustache on his face with a piece of coal.

"Ladies and gents! Stand out your ears! Today you will see, *right before your eyes*, the amazing, the mystifying, the utterly unbelievable Disappearing Trunk Trick." Saulie pulls down the blanket with a big *swoosh*. Both coatracks and the broom handle crash to the floor. "Ignore that!" he shouts, as he steps over the racks to get to the trunk.

The "trunk" is a crooked box he hammered

together out of two wooden crates, the whole thing resting on a couple of sawed-off stools. There's a loose drape of fabric nailed along the bottom edge of the box to make like a hidden space beneath the trunk. (He didn't even bother to hem!) The whole thing looks like a boat that's about to go under, and I don't like the idea of Zelda crawling into it. She could get a splinter, or worse.

Saulie shows us how good the trunk is. He turns it every which way, knocking on the sides with his wooden cane to show there are no holes.

"And now," he says. "May I introduce my assistant, Miss Zelda Rosenfeld!"

Zelda has been waiting in the kitchen to make her big entrance. She jumps into the doorway, wearing the costume I made: red stockings, white slippers, and a white muslin cap-sleeved tunic that's tied at the waist with a red satin sash. She waves to us, then blows me a kiss. My heart turns over on itself. We all applaud, and Mrs. Pelz leans over to me and whispers, "Like an angel from heaven, this child is to me."

"And now, let the magic begin," says Saulie. "Watch carefully as I wrap my lovely assistant, Miss Zelda Rosenfeld, in this velvet cape." Saulie wraps Zelda in an old cotton sheet. Only her legs stick out at the bottom. "And now! Into the Disappearing Trunk she goes!" He helps Zelda climb into the wooden crate and closes the flimsy lid on top of her. Then he sets up the two coat racks and hangs up the curtain again, so the box, we can't see.

I don't like this part. I know it's just a crazy contraption that Saulie hammered together in the alley behind the building, but it looks too much like a coffin to me. What if Zelda pokes her eye on something? What if her hair gets snagged? What if the whole thing collapses and she gets a cut or a bruise? I dig my fingernails into the palm of my hand, wishing the show was over.

During the next bit, Saulie talks extra loud, and there's some banging and bumping noises from behind the curtain. After a couple of minutes, everything goes quiet. Saulie looks behind, then comes back out front.

"And now, ladies and gents," he says, "prepare to be amazed." He unhooks the curtain and lets it fall to the floor. "You see the trunk, exactly as I left it. And now, I will reach *into* the trunk and pull out . . ." Saulie reaches down into the trunk and pulls out—just the sheet, which he waves over his head. ". . . the velvet cape! But where is the lovely Miss Zelda Rosenfeld? See for yourself!"

He tips the wooden crate so we can see. It's empty.

Mrs. Pelz applauds wildly, and Mama and I clap, too. It really is a very good trick, and I'm impressed that Saulie and Zelda pulled it off. But mostly I'm just relieved that it's over and Zelda didn't get crushed. You never know what can happen in such a thing as a Disappearing Trunk.

"Take a bow, *Zeldaleh*!" calls out Mrs. Pelz. "You did good! Come take a bow, Little One!" We keep up the applause while we wait for Zelda to crawl out from under the trunk. But she doesn't come, and I think, *Oy gevalt, she hit her head and is lying on the floor, out cold!*

"Saulie!" I say sternly. "Make to bring her out!" Saulie stops his bowing long enough to fish under the trunk. He lifts up the fabric and bends down low. Then he stands up sudden-like and rubs his face nervously. Half of his charcoal mustache turns into a grayish smear that reaches from under his nose to his neck.

"She ain't there," he croaks.

"Wha'd'ya mean?" I say, getting out of my seat. I bend down and scrabble aside the fabric. There's nothing underneath except for the two sawed-off stools.

"What have you done with her?" I shout at Saulie.

Saulie looks wild-eyed. "She's supposed to be there," he says, pointing at the space below the trunk. "She drops out the bottom and then waits for the act to be over. We rehearsed it! She's gone. Really gone!"

I'm walking all around the trunk like a crazy person with her head on fire. How can she be gone? She was just here a minute ago. I saw her with my own eyes. The red tights, the white slippers, her beautiful smile—they were all here a minute ago. How can she be gone like that in an instant?

"You bring her back!" I shout at Saulie. "You bring her back this instant, mister!" I'm remembering that time on Delancey Street. I'm remembering the horses and wagons clattering past, and the dark hole that kept getting bigger and bigger until I nearly fell in.

Saulie shrugs his shoulders up to his ears. "It's magic! I don't know how from nothin'! She really disappeared this time. Not just a trick!"

"You bring her back!" I scream. I start to hit Saulie on the side of the head. Mrs. Pelz jumps up and tries to calm me down. How can a person just disappear like that—*pfffft*—into thin air? How did I lose her, so quick like that?

We are all standing and looking now. Mama walks straight to the window and looks out on the fire escape and down at the street below. But it's Mrs. Pelz who puts two and two together and lifts the lid of the blanket box against the wall. "Essie," she calls out sharply. "Only look!"

When I turn, Zelda pops up like a jack-in-the-box just sprung. "Ta-da!" she shouts, flinging both her arms over her head and wiggling her hips. She's looking at me and wanting something. I know what it is, but I can't say anything. I think I've swallowed my own tongue.

"Only *say*, Essie," she pouts. "Say like you always do."

I know what she wants. Our game. "Oh, it's you," I manage to scratch out, and then she smiles and jumps out of the box and dances over to me.

I look at Saulie, and now I see the smile that creeps over his face and tells me that he knew all along where Zelda was.

"A little joke, Essie," he says, seeing how mad I

still am. "What? You never played a little joke?"

I'm ready to rush at him again, but Zelda is all wrapped up in my skirts. "I was great, Essie!" she says. "Tell me I was great!" She wants to be picked up and petted.

So I do. I gather her up in my arms—still I can hold her, even though she's five—and tell her she is the most wonderful magician's assistant that ever lived, and if she ever, *ever* disappears like that again, I will lock her up in my own special box and never let her out.

Chapter 9

BY THE TIME I GOT HOME, IT WAS ALL FIGHTING and accusations. Mama shouting it was my fault Saulie got nicked. "You, always saying he would end up in The Tombs, now look what you done!" Then Freyda ticking her finger back and forth in front of Mama's face. "Essie's fault? Essie's fault? She's not his mama!" And Mrs. Pelz closing her eyes and breathing out, "It's a judgment from God, is what, because we hadn't kept the *Shabbos* since Papa died."

And all the time Mama pulling on her hair, pulling out pieces of her own hair, pacing back and forth across the kitchen floor, whispering, "My son. My only son."

And me thinking of Saulie and thinking, *He's locked up. Locked in a room with no windows, no light. Locked up like he's some kind of animal what doesn't have a mind and a heart that bleeds.*

If Jimmy hadn't walked in then, I don't know what would have happened. We were half out of our minds. "Mrs. Pelz?" he said, standing in the open door, not sure if he should come in.

It was decided that me and Jimmy would go to The Tombs together to try to get Saulie out. When I turned to leave, Mama grabbed my arm and said, "You bring him back." She gave my arm a little shake. "You bring him back to me." It wasn't a plea. It was a threat.

"I promise, Mama," I said. I was shaking like a wet cat, but I tried to sound strong and brave. Somebody had to, and there weren't any other volunteers.

Halfway down our block, Jimmy said, "Take my arm." I put my hand through the crook of his elbow, and Jimmy pulled it in tight to his body so suddenly I felt anchored, where before I'd been like a boat cut loose. "You don't need to hurry," said Jimmy. "He isn't going anywhere." I realized I'd been half-running, but now I slowed my step to match Jimmy's steady pace.

The Tombs is the worst place you could end up, unless you count the bottom of the East River, and even then I'm not sure which is worse. Four floors high and made out of stone with round towers like something in a witch's story, it took up a whole city block. Just looking at it made the hairs on the back of my neck prickle up.

I'd walked by the outside before, but I'd never been in.

The horror stories, though—those I'd heard. About the cells dug deep underground. About the dark that never changed, night or day. About the walls running with water. About the rats the size of cats. About the one bucket in the corner for twenty prisoners to use. The food was bread and water, if you were lucky. The cops beat you just because they were bored. You had to sleep standing up or else you'd end up crawling with lice.

I couldn't bear to think of Saulie down there, rats creeping up his legs, cops hitting him with their sticks. When we got to the steps leading up to the front door, I said, "Stop. Just a minute." Then I closed my eyes and said a quick prayer. It wouldn't do any good—I knew it wouldn't—but I said it anyway.

I wanted to have faith. But faith in what? I didn't know.

Faith in God? Faith in Jimmy?

Just faith.

And part of faith is the *doing* of the thing—saying the prayer, lighting the candles, reading the words—*doing* even before the *believing* happens. So I said my prayer on the steps of The Tombs—"Please God, help me bring my brother home tonight"—and then we walked in.

Jimmy knew where to go without asking. He'd been here before with other lawyer students. He led me into a large room with hundreds of people, then pointed to a long wooden bench that ran the whole length of a wall. "Have a seat, Essie. There's a line to talk to the desk sergeant. It'll be a long wait."

"I'll wait with," I said, still holding tight to his arm.

"There's no point," he said, uncurling my fingers from his elbow. "Sit down, and I'll keep my eye on you. As soon as I get to the front of the line, you can come and stand with me."

This is part of having faith, I told myself. I went to the bench and sat myself down next to an old woman with no teeth who smelled like horse-radish.

The room was huge and all lit up with electric lights attached to long wires that hung from the ceiling. I stared up. The ceiling was two stories above my head. The floor was stone, which made the room echo. Voices from every corner seemed to bounce like balls set loose in a back alley. On the wall behind me were notices—hundreds of them—with pictures and written descriptions of people. Some were marked "Missing," and others were marked "Wanted." It was like having a gallery of ghosts watching me over my shoulder.

I wrapped my shawl tight around me and waited. Ten minutes went by. Then another ten. Jimmy was moving up the line slowly. Who knew there'd be so many people in line at seven o'clock on a Thursday evening? I wondered how many crooks and hoodlums the police arrested every day. A hundred? Two hundred? Three? So many families come to get their boys out of jail. So many boys lost on the streets of New York.

I stood up and straightened my skirt. It hung too loose around my waist, all because I'd lost my appetite lately. I sat down again. The old woman next to me fell asleep. Sleeping, she snapped her toothless gums together. I smoothed my skirt over my knees. As I ran my hand down the side of my leg, I felt something in my side pocket. I reached my hand in and pulled out the piece of newspaper that I'd stashed away last week.

LOST

There it was, that same headline: LOST. So small on the page. Just one word, all of four letters. The woman next to me began to snore, a tuneless hum that marked my progress as I read through the article.

LOST

The hope, shared until lately by nearly everybody who reads the newspapers, that Miss Dorothy Arnold was living and would soon be found was based on reasonable grounds. If she had been kidnapped for ransom the kidnappers would surely have tried long before this to get money. If she had been murdered, the band of Pinkerton detectives and the police of many cities would have found some clue to her murderers even if they had not found her body. There has been no justification to the theory of murder. Yet the reasonable foundations of hope have been sapped. Miss Arnold is lost, as it seems hopelessly lost, and not a single useful clue to the means of her disappearance has been discovered in three months. District Attorney Whitman's official effort to discover what substance there may be in the assertions of some persons that they know something about her disappearance is not likely to have any substantial outcome.

The family, when they made public the fact of her disappearance, concealed from the police some investigations they had been making privately, an unwise course, but perfectly natural and understandable. When this became known, the police became incredulous and the public mind was bewildered. Yet then, as now, the only significant facts concerning Miss Arnold's disappearance were her departure from home Dec. 12 on a shopping errand, her purchase of a book, her meeting with an acquaintance on Fifth Avenue to whom she remarked that she was going to walk in Central Park on her way home, her purchase of a box of candy. The statement that she applied for letters that day at the General Post Office lacks positive verification, and so does the testimony that she had made inquiries touching the sailing of ships to foreign ports. Neither seems, at this time, of much significance. These and other statements, which have helped to confuse the matter were withheld until late in the day, when the loss of Miss Arnold had become an absorbing news subject.

Searchers for a lost object invariably begin the search systematically, discarding improbable clues, but in a prolonged search all system disappears, the most fantastic theories seem worth following, judgment is overcome by anxiety. The latest seeming "developments" turn out to be no developments at all. The journey to Italy of her mother and brother was obviously fruitless. Her friends were still indulging a faint, agonized hope that she might be somewhere in hiding. They have been calling, vainly calling, that is all. The detectives followed all sorts of futile clues, and the discovery of the clues by others led to vain conjectures. The fictitious structure of romance, suspicion, and gossip is fading away. The public begins to see that no logical explanation of Miss Arnold's intentional disappearance has been revealed, that no fact concerning her which her family tried to withhold from the public was of the slightest relative importance. She was not over-romantic or morbid or eccentric. In the heart of a city of 5,000,000 inhabitants, on a fair day in December, she disappeared. It seems not unlikely that her case will be another of those unsolved mysteries which, from time to time, unsettle public confidence in the machinery of modern civilization.

Yes. I *did* remember the story.

Dorothy Arnold had been walking down Fifth Avenue on a cold, sunny December day, shopping for a dress for her sister's coming-out party. She'd stopped at Park & Tilford's and bought a box of candy. She'd stopped at Brentano's and bought a book. Outside the store on 27th Street, she'd bumped into a friend and they'd talked for a bit about a party that weekend they were both invited to. Then she'd headed back up Fifth Avenue on her way home. But instead of going home, she'd vanished.

If she'd been just anyone—a shoe clerk, a cab driver, an East-Sider—the story would have stopped there. But Dorothy Arnold was the daughter of a millionaire. She lived with her parents in a mansion on East 79th Street. Her uncle was a former Supreme Court judge. The Arnold family was socially prominent and regularly made the society pages of *The New York Times*.

She wasn't just anyone.

It's like if you're on a street corner and someone next to you says, "I lost a penny," you would take a look around and do your best to help find it. Sure, you would. But if someone on that same corner says, "I lost a diamond ring," you would get down on your hands and knees and search 'til the sun went down. And the next day, you'd come back and start looking all over again. And then every time you passed that corner, you'd think to yourself, "I wonder if they ever found that diamond ring," and I bet your eyes would wander to the ground and have another look. For years and years.

Dorothy Arnold was a diamond ring, and the country had gone wild looking for her.

There were many strange things about the story, I remembered. The secret boyfriend, older and jowly, who was in Italy when she disappeared, but then came back and said he would find her and marry her. The father, insisting she was dead long before the police gave up their investigation. Her family's secrecy, not telling anyone she had disappeared for six weeks before finally calling the police. How could you expect to find anyone then?

"You can't sit here!" said a sharp voice as a wooden stick banged down on the bench.

I jumped to my feet, accidentally ripping the

newspaper in my hand. But it wasn't me the police-man was talking to with his nightstick. It was the old woman. "Get on with ya," he said, poking the old lady like she had lice. "No sleeping in the sta-tion. Out you go."

The old woman didn't say a word. I had the feeling this was nothing new for her. She stood up and started for the door. When she passed me, she gave me a wink and, quick as a cat, she blew me a kiss. It made me reel back, like I'd been slapped. Wish or curse, who could tell?

After she was gone, I was left alone with my thoughts.

There's a part of our minds that's hidden from ourselves. There are secret memories, deep inside our brains, that make us do things and say things — like we're puppets who don't have free will. Scientists have figured this out, alienists who study the human mind. I read a book once by a famous German alienist, and he said the mind is *not* a shin-ing light. The mind is *not* an open book. It's a deep, dark cellar where rats and spiders and snakes con-stantly fight each other. And everything that hap-pens in the cellar happens for one of two reasons: the desire to make new life, or the need to run from death.

I read a whole book about this. Jimmy never read that one. He said it didn't interest him.

Standing in The Tombs, in that great stone hall lit up by a hundred electric lights, I could sense the catacomb beneath my feet. The dark tunnels, the dirt floors, the locked doors, the tortured souls.

And in my brain, I knew something that I didn't know. Something I'd known for weeks. Something I'd kept at the edge of my vision, always just out of sight. Something I'd kept in the dark, hidden from myself.

The rats and spiders and snakes were crawling up the cellar steps.

Jimmy was at the front of the line. My eyes watched as he talked to the desk sergeant. I should be up there, finding out about my brother. But instead I turned around and faced the wall of faces, the ghosts of all the missing and wanted.

It was like looking through a family album, looking at each face with a "hmm" and an "oh," before going on to the next. There were hundreds, and I rested my eyes on each one before moving on.

When I finally reached her photograph, there wasn't even a moment of surprise. There she was, just like I knew she would be, just like part of me had been waiting for her to appear.

"Oh, it's you," I said, very quietly.

There were three photographs of Harriet, and in each one she looked beautiful. Here she was in a smart walking costume. And here in evening dress. And last, a bust portrait, where she's wearing the most gorgeous basin hat I had ever seen—enormous, velvety, and banded with two silk roses. In that picture, she looked serious and maybe even sad. But she also looked a little stuck-up, the way the rich do.

Underneath the three photographs, there was a description.

LOST

DOROTHY HARRIET CAMILLE ARNOLD

When she left home she was dressed as follows:

A tailor-made, plain blue serge suit, the coat reaching about to the hips, and cut in at the waist; the skirt was cut straight; black velvet hat, with small irregular brim and a baker's crown, trimmed with two blue silk roses, Alice blue lining, maker's name Genevieve; underclothing was fine tailor-made, Minnie Hinck, maker, although the maker's name was probably not on it; low-cut black shoes, from the Walkover Company; black silk stockings; waist of dark blue cloth, same as suit, and dark blue chiffon, with neck cut V-shape, and Irish lace at the neck where it was cut low, and probably a jabot. She also wore tan walking gloves. The hair was worn in a very full pompadour and far down on forehead. Shell hair comb, and carved barrette; hatpin and drop earrings of blue lapis lazuli.

She carried a large black fox flat muff with white points, but no other furs, and carried a black velvet handbag, containing about $20 or $30, cards, and possibly other papers of various kinds.

The last trace which can be found of her was a short while after she left home, when she was seen at Brentano's and at Park & Tilford's Fifty-Ninth Street store.

No reasons are known to her family which would induce her to leave her home nor is there any indication of such intent on her part. A liberal reward will be paid for information leading to the discovery of her whereabouts.

JAMES C. CROPSEY
Police Commissioner

"The bail is set at fifty dollars," said Jimmy.

I jumped. Fifty dollars! It was more money than God carried in his pocket. "Can't you talk him down?" I asked.

Jimmy looked tired. He shook his head. "Bail's set by the judge, not the desk sergeant. Saulie'll have his hearing tomorrow. Or Monday. The desk sergeant said they're pretty backed up. 'Like the sewers,' is what he said."

"Monday!" I said. I counted off the days. "That's four days. He can't stay locked up 'til Monday!"

"Fifty bucks, it's a lot of money, Essie."

It was a fortune. I started adding in my head. I had my secret fund, twelve whole dollars saved over a year. And there was the rent money in the cracker tin, due next week, but the rent would have to wait. Did Mrs. Pelz have a little to spare? Maybe Freyda's mama could give a dollar or two?

The numbers jumped in my head, but they didn't add up to fifty dollars. There was only one person I knew who had that kind of money.

"Jimmy," I said. "Will you come with me and not ask any questions? Just come with me and wait outside a door while I talk to someone?"

"Sure, Essie," he said, putting a hand on my shoulder. His eyes were warm and kind. "I'd do anything for you."

LOST

Was he really saying such a thing to me? I let his words sink into my heart and light me up for just a minute. Then I took his arm again, and Jimmy and me, we left the garishly bright Tombs and headed out into the night.

January 9, 1911

The lace on my boot snaps in two. Ach! I take off
the boot and hold it on my lap, while I tie the two
ends of the lace together. Zelda walks into the
kitchen and comes over to the chair where I'm sitting. I don't even look up, I'm not talking to her the
way she's acting. She stands in front of me for a
minute and then throws her beanbag at me. It hits
me square in the chest and lands in my lap on top
of the boot I'm trying to fix.

"Quit it," I say, tossing the beanbag on the
floor. I don't even look up. She stomps her foot and
kicks the leg of the chair.

"*Quit it*, I said! *Nu!*" I give her a *klop* on the *kop*
so she'll know I mean business. Saulie's asleep in
the parlor, but we don't need to keep our voices
down. He could sleep through an explosion.

Zelda's been like this all morning. My hair is
ready to run off my head, I'm so irritated.

"You. Stay. Home," she says, giving the chair a
swift kick with each word.

I put my hands on her shoulders. "I can't," I
say. "I have to go to work, like Mama does. Like
you will, someday. Everybody works, Zelda."

"Not you!" she says, her voice rising to a
scream. "You stay home with me!"

Mama walks in from the bedroom, dressed and
ready herself. She got special permission from her
boss at the bakery to come to work late today so
she could help me out the door.

"You see what you done?" she says, going to
the cold box. "Every little thing, she makes like the

world is coming to an end." She cuts off a wedge of cheese and slices a piece of bread, then wraps each up in a piece of newspaper and drops the bundles in a string bag—my dinner for my first day at work.

"Mama," I say, finishing with my boot. "Don't start with the lecture."

"I'm just saying," says Mama. "Every little thing."

"Yeah, yeah," I say. I'll go crazy out of my head with all the things I'm thinking and feeling. I wonder how it will be at the factory, if I can keep up, what the girls will be like. Freyda says it's hard work and the bosses are cruel, but that the girls are loads of fun. I think it will be an adventure. Something new. And even though I can hardly stand the thought of leaving Zelda all day, I'm a little excited. And nervous. Confused.

I'm all dressed. Last night, Mama washed and ironed my blouse and brushed my skirt, hanging everything neat and clean over the back of a kitchen chair. Now my dinner is ready. The only thing left is for me to put on my hat and shawl.

"Mama, my new hat, have you seen?"

"Always a new one," mutters Mama. "I put it in the parlor, so it wouldn't get *farpotshket*."

I go into the parlor, but the hat, it isn't there. So I go into the bedroom, and there's Zelda on the bed, wearing the hat and tossing her beanbag like it's just another day.

"Zelda, give me the hat," I say, standing in the doorway.

"No," she says.

"Zelda, I mean business!" I grab for the hat, but Zelda is as fast as a rabbit. She scooches to the other side of the bed, just out of my reach. *Oy, vey!*

My clothes are all nice and clean. I don't want to get them rumpled up in a chase. I think on what Jimmy always says: "There's more than one way to skin a cat." So I sit on the bed with my back to her, and I say, "Zelda, I gotta go to work, even without my hat. I wish I could look good for my first day, though. Do you want the other girls to laugh at your sister Essie what shows up with no hat on her head?"

Zelda creeps up behind me as quiet as she can. Gentle as a butterfly, she places the hat on my head. Then she throws her arms around my neck and cries, "Don't go!"

It breaks my heart in two, and I feel like the smallest crumb under the kitchen table for being even a little happy that I am starting work. I reach behind me and wrap my arms around her and give her a little bounce. "*Sha*," I say. "*Sha, Zeldaleh*. We all gotta work. It isn't fair to Mama."

"I hate Mama," she whimpers into my neck.

"No, Zelda! Never say!"

"I do. I do. And she hates me!" says Zelda, squeezing my neck so hard I think I am like to choke to death.

"No, it isn't true," I say. "No mama hates her *kinder*. It isn't possible. Come here." I pull her around to the front of me and settle her on my lap. "When mamas have babies, it's like the whole world lights up. But then, there's so much worry and work to take care of a baby, it's hard for the mamas to always remember the light of that joy. So the babies, they have to work hard to be extra good, to help the mamas remember the joy. Can you do that? Be extra good?"

Zelda looks very sad and serious on my lap. Then she shakes her head *no*.

What did I expect, trying to fool her in with that cockamamie story? I squeeze her so hard she squeals. "Zelda, I'm only sixteen and you're giving me the gray hairs already!"

"I'm going to hide!" she says, like it's a new idea that has just popped into her head. "I'm going to hide every single morning so you can't find me. Then you'll feel bad every time you go to work and you'll stop going."

"Zelda, don't!" I say, but she has already wriggled out of my arms and is running into the kitchen to find one of her favorite hiding spots. I follow but haven't got time to be searching all over the flat for her. "Zelda!"

"Let her go," says Mama. "You're going to be late."

She's right, and even I know you can't be late to the Triangle. I pick up my dinner and put on my shawl.

Out on the street, Freyda is fit to be tied. "If you want to be late, that's your business, but don't make me late, too!" She yanks her arm through mine, and we start to run, me looking over my shoulder to see if maybe Zelda crawled out onto the fire escape to wave goodbye.

But there's no one there.

Chapter 10

IT WAS EIGHT O'CLOCK WHEN WE REACHED Harriet's apartment, and I expected a light to be on, but her windows were dark. Jimmy was as good as his word and didn't ask even one question, just said, "I'll wait for you right here. Shout if you need me." Then he crossed his arms and leaned against the stone baluster at the bottom of Harriet's steps. I knew he'd stay there. All night if he had to.

I went up the stairs and into her building, wondering if she was out for the evening. But where would she have gone, all by herself? I was about to knock on her door, then stopped, worried that a noise might call the neighbors. On the East Side, when somebody knocks on a door everyone on the hallway opens theirs, just to see who it is. East-Siders are nosy like that, and I was used to it. But here? I didn't want any nosy neighbors here. Not tonight.

Instead, I flipped back the torn carpeting in the corner and picked up Harriet's spare key. I slipped it in the lock and opened the door, then put the key back in its hiding place. Quiet as a mouse crossing a grave, I let myself into Harriet's dark apartment.

Everything about the room felt different. The drapes, pulled shut, looked heavy and suffocating. The piano hulked in the corner. The fireplace was a bruise. The doorway to the kitchen had the feeling of a dark alley late at night.

Looking around, I tried to remember the sound of our laughter, the way Harriet and I had sat on the sofa—that one, right there—night after night, and talked and joked and become friends. But the sound of our laughter was buried in these dead and darkened walls. I couldn't pull it out. I couldn't lift it up.

Harriet wasn't Harriet. Her name was Dorothy. Even now I couldn't make that name stick in my mind when I pictured her face. She wasn't a poor factory worker, like me. She had millions. She wasn't struggling to survive. If life got too hard, she could walk uptown to her family's mansion. Was there a single thing she'd told me that I could believe?

What was true and what was false? I didn't know, so it made *everything* seem like a lie. The friendship was an illusion, a magician's trick, a sleight of hand. I felt myself disappearing in this room, turning invisible. Harriet was a mirage. I had never even existed here.

I held up my hand in front of my face. It was gray, shadowy, the edges indistinct. If I moved it far enough away, it seemed to vanish.

My eyes looked beyond my hand to the curtained windows and something that seemed to hang in the air in front of them. It was white and floating, and seemed almost to glow in the smothery gloom.

Was it a ghost? I didn't believe. What could it

be? My eyes played tricks on me, and I thought I saw the thing move. Slowly, I worked my way across the room.

It was a white lace tablecloth spread across the small, round table.

Harriet had begun to set the table for the tea party on Sunday. I rested my hand on the tablecloth and ran my fingertips along the thin, interwoven strings. Every cross, every twist, every knot had been made by the hands of some woman, somewhere in some time. Working with bobbins and thread, she had done what her mother had done and her grandmother had done and her great-grandmother before that: creating something out of nothing, looping together pieces to make something whole. Something that would last beyond the grave.

In the dark, my hands felt across the top of the lace-covered table and found the first teacup and then the second and third. Already stationed. Ready for the party that would never happen. It broke my heart to smash that picture in my head, the picture of Zelda here in this apartment and all of us laughing and singing and dancing. It broke my heart.

There was a sound from the bedroom, a muffled rustle. I froze, my hand still on the rim of one of the teacups. I had thought I was alone.

Through the blackness, I made my way to the bedroom. I leaned into the room and called out softly.

"Harriet? It's me, Essie." I looked into the dark

and windowless room. It was impossible to tell if there was someone on the bed. I could barely see five feet ahead of me. "Harriet?"

"What?" said a voice pulled out of sleep.

"It's me, Essie. I need to talk to you."

"Essie?" said Harriet. Now I could see the gray outline of her sitting up in bed. "What time is it?"

"About eight o'clock."

"Oh," she said. "I was so tired when I got home from work. I didn't even eat supper. I just crawled into bed."

"Is there a lamp in here?"

"On the table," she said. "Do you mind lighting it? You know how I hate to strike a match."

I found my way to the table and lit the lamp. The room sketched itself in. Harriet was in bed, sitting up, but with the covers pulled up to her chin. In all the time I'd known her, I'd never seen her with her hair down, but now it was unpinned and reached to her waist. Tangled from sleep, it made her look even younger. In the indistinct light, she could have been fourteen.

Harriet looked at my face. "Are you all right?" she asked.

I sat down on the bed and told myself to sharpen up. This was going to be easy or this was going to be hard, but no matter what, I was leaving with the bail money in my hand.

"I need fifty dollars. Tonight."

"Are you in trouble? Is somebody after you?"

"My brother Saulie's in jail. I need to get him out."

"Oh, Essie. How awful. What did he do?"

"It doesn't matter," I said, impatience puncturing my voice. "I need the money. Right now."

"From me, you mean?" she said. She looked confused. "I haven't got fifty dollars. You can have whatever's in my purse, but there's hardly . . . I haven't got fifty dollars."

"Then you have to get it. Tonight," I said. "I need to bring my brother home tonight."

Harriet raised her eyebrows. "I can't think of how I could get —"

I put my hands on her shoulders and shook her hard. "I know who you are!" I said. "You're Dorothy Arnold. Your father has millions of dollars. I need fifty of them. Tonight."

Harriet looked at me like time had just stopped. Her eyes grew wide and her mouth opened slightly. She shook her head. "I'm not . . . No, I'm not . . ." she murmured.

"Stop lying!" I said, shaking her again. "Stop lying to me. Everything you told me was a lie. All of it." I turned away from her, afraid that I might strike her.

Her eyes filled. "It wasn't, Essie," she said. "It wasn't a lie. It was more true than anything in my whole life." She reached across the blanket and tried to take my hand, but I wouldn't let her.

"Just stop it," I said. "Stop with your novels and your 'truth.' I'm sick to death of it. Enough already with the books and the music and the tea parties! I need *money*. And I need it tonight."

"You can take anything," she said, looking

around the room. "Anything I have. Sell it all—"

I pointed a finger at her. "There's a reward out for you," I said. "Did you know that?" Harriet's face changed. It was like she'd still been asleep and now she was finally waking up. "A thousand dollars. It said in the papers. All I have to do is tell them where you are."

Harriet's voice shook. "Would you do that?"

A thousand dollars. A thousand dollars. I thought of everything that meant. Saulie out of jail. No more worries about the rent. A flat with hot and cold water and a bathroom we didn't share. A hat shop of my own. Books for Zelda, as many as she wanted . . . .

"Essie, you're shaking," said Harriet. "Put this blanket around you."

"I don't need a blanket," I said, pushing it aside. "I need to get my brother out of jail. He's locked up. Locked in a room with no windows. With rats crawling all around him." I grabbed her again and gave her a violent shake. "I can't lose him."

I had tried so hard not to cry, but this last broke me. *Enough already,* said my heart. *Enough.* I cried the way I had when Papa died. Great heaving sobs that felt like I would bring up my guts, a vomiting of tears and misery.

Harriet sat beside me with one arm around my waist. "No, no," she murmured. "You won't lose him. I promise. He's going to be fine. Everything's going to be fine." She stroked my head. It was like the times Zelda sat on my bed during my monthly sickness and patted me on the cheek and told me the pain would be gone soon, soon.

My crying turned to hiccups. The hiccups finally faded away. I said, "Oh, Harriet. Can't you just go home? Your family's sick with worry over you. Whatever you did, can't you go back to them?"

"I can't," she said. "They don't want me, anyway."

"They do!" I said. "Always in the papers, they're saying how your mama won't leave the house and your papa cries the River Jordan every time he says your name. They're heartbroken."

She shook her head. "It's an act," said Harriet. "It is! A play they're putting on for the whole world to watch. They don't want me back. They're glad I'm gone."

"That can't be true."

"It is true. All of them, except maybe John. I don't know for sure. I'm too afraid to find out."

I couldn't believe what she was saying. "A brother *always* takes care of his sister."

"My family's not like yours," said Harriet. "There are so many rules where I come from. It's not like here. Where I come from, if you break the rules, they throw you out."

"Family is family."

"You don't understand," said Harriet. "I'm glad you don't. It's a good thing." She got up off the bed, pulling the blanket around her so it hung like a cape from her shoulders. "Bring the lamp."

I followed her into the parlor. She opened the writing desk, and I watched as she plucked the bird off its nest and retrieved the hidden key. In a minute, she was saying, "Take these," and handed me the earrings and the hatpin from the locked drawer.

They were, I suspected, the last things she had from her family. The very last gifts from her parents. The last tie to that other life of hers. In my hand, they were cold and hard. I ran one finger along the metal of the hatpin and felt the sharp prick of the tip. A hatpin like that could kill. I wondered if it wounded her, giving them up like this.

But all she said was, "They're worth two hundred dollars, maybe more. You can get at least thirty, probably forty for them. I didn't sell them before because they were in the papers so much, and they're unusual, so I thought they'd cause suspicion. Be careful when you sell them."

I nodded. I would be careful.

My eyes caught sight of an envelope resting on top of the desk. In Harriet's peculiar script, the name "Zelda" was written on it. Harriet followed my eye. She picked up the envelope and didn't seem to know what to say about it.

"Would you . . . ?" She paused, then held the envelope out for me to take. "Would you give this to Zelda for me? I want her to have a proper invitation."

I took the envelope. It was crisp and smooth in my hand, the corners as sharp as a knife's point. I slipped it into my pocket. Then I pulled out my limp handkerchief from my waistband and wrapped up the earrings and the hatpin so they wouldn't be in plain view.

At the door, I stopped. "I don't know what to

call you anymore."

"Liar? Fraud? Ingrate?" she said with a wry smile. "Take your pick."

"That's not what I meant," I said.

"Call me Harriet. I'm really not Dorothy anymore."

I looked at her. Who was this Mystery Woman? I didn't know.

"Thank you, Harriet."

"You're welcome," she said. Then she put a hand on my elbow and asked, "Are you going to turn me in?"

I didn't say anything. I looked her in the eye. She gave my arm a little squeeze. "No lies," she said.

I thought of the hat shop and a clean place to live and freedom from the thousand-and-one worries that poverty brings. There would be money for a doctor when we needed one and the rent always ready at the end of the month and maybe we could even take a little trip to the country in the summer when the heat in the city was killing. And I thought of Harriet's family and how they grieved for her. No one should feel grief like that.

"I don't know," I said. "I don't know."

She nodded then, and kissed my cheek, and wished me *good luck*.

And I left her like that. Just like that.

February 6, 1911

It's Zelda's sixth birthday, and she's wound up like a top. She should have been in bed an hour ago—we all should have. But there's still the laundry to do, and I wanted to work on the hat I'd promised her, and just when Zelda was in her nightdress and her face washed and her hair pulled into a braid, Jimmy stuck his head in the door, home late from night classes, and said he had a present for her.

So now she's next door and we can hear her shouting and laughing, and Mama's at the sink, filling the wash boiler for a second load of whites, and I've just finished crimping the last of the support wires for the brim, but there's still all the joins to finish and trim. We'll be up past midnight at this rate.

"Essie, stop with the hat and give a hand," says Mama. With both of us working now, the laundry only gets done in the evenings, which means there are wet clothes strung up most nights during the week. I get up from the table and help her lift the boiler to the stove. It weighs fifty pounds, and the cold water sloshes over the sides and soaks our skirts.

I go back to the table and sit down. The hat I'm making is a Merry Widow, the first ever for me. It's an enormous hat—you could house a family of five under the brim—and I don't know how Zelda's going to keep it on her head, but she's been begging me for one for months. I should have started it weeks ago, but working in the factory means there's never enough time for anything else. And now it's her birthday, and I'm just beginning.

"Put away that," says Mama. "I need the help with the laundry."

"Just half an hour, Mama," I say. "I want to finish the frame. Just that." Maybe tomorrow I'll have time to hunt for the black organdy in Chinatown. Maybe I can convince Freyda to come with.

"Ridiculous, that hat," Mama grumbles. "You feed her with these ideas. Always these crazy ideas. She's gonna be a Broadway star some day. *Pfff!* I tell you what. She's gonna be a factory worker, is what she's gonna be."

"You never know," I say. I hate this talk from Mama. Always the black side of things.

"*I* know. Believe me, I know." She snaps out the wet clothes and hangs them across the line strung from one end of the room to the other. My chemise and two underskirts. Zelda's nightgown. Saulie's drawers. They float like ghosts in the gray kitchen light.

The door flies open and Zelda blows in. "Only look, Essie! From Jimmy!" She holds up a half-eaten stick of candied tangerine slices. Flecks of sugar fly off as she waves the stick like a marching baton.

"Zelda, to bed," says Mama, her words mumbled by the clothes peg in her mouth.

"You want one?" she asks, holding the stick up to Mama.

"*Ach!* No! The sugar on the clothes, Zelda! To

keep them clean, please. Take away. Take away!"
Mama shoos Zelda away from her pile of clean
whites, and Zelda sashays over to me.

"Essie, you like a little?" She holds the stick in
front of my mouth.

I lift my eyebrows and smile. Zelda slides a
slice off the stick and drops it into my open mouth.
The sudden sweet makes my saliva run so that my
mouth cramps up with an ache just under my ears.
It's delicious.

Zelda leans in close and whispers in my ear,
"For you, two!" and then pops a second slice into
my mouth. I laugh.

She looks at the hat frame. "Will it be done
tonight?" she asks.

"No, not tonight. I told you."

"You're so slow!" she complains, licking her
fingers that are sticky and smeared with orange. "I
want to show Jimmy! Hurry up!"

"Zelda," says Mama. "You're a mess. *Kommen.*"

"No!" shrieks Zelda, and runs out of the room
and back into Mrs. Pelz's flat.

My head is bent over my work, and Mama is at
the stove when I say it. It's like someone else's voice
in the room.

"Why do you hate her so much?"

When my ears hear these words, I can't believe
they came out of my own mouth. It's a question I've
asked in my head a dozen times, but never I said it
out loud before.

"You don't know nothing from hate," Mama
says. Quiet. "This is hate?" she asks, pointing at the

clothes hanging on the line. "This?" She waves her hand at the kitchen. She bends over the soak tub and begins to scrub against the washboard. "You think love is all white dresses and picture hats and ice cream cones. You don't know nothing from love."

Zelda runs in again, making more noise than a marching band. She is overtired and has a wild look in her eyes. She high-steps through the room, holding the empty stick from her tangerine slices over her head. "Who wants to lick the stick?" she shouts. "Mama? Essie? You want a lick?" The wooden stick glistens with sugar crystals and the slick, leftover gumminess of the candied fruit.

"Zelda!" shouts Mama. "Look at your face! I just washed. Come here. Come here and get wiped right now!"

"No!" says Zelda, climbing onto my lap. "I won't."

"No? What kind of a child?" says Mama. She wets a rag in the slop sink and comes toward us. "Don't you say 'no' to me."

"Mama," I say, trying to get her to stop already. "Let me. I can do."

"No!" says Mama. "You spoil her. Always she gets her way. She is the *child*, and she will do what I tell her."

"Mama, not now," I say. "It's late. Everybody's tired. Just for tonight, let me do. Here. Give to me the rag. I'll do." I stretch out my hand. If she will give it to me, I can warm it in the wash water, and then Zelda won't mind so much a gentle wipe on the face.

But Mama won't stop. She pushes the rag toward

Zelda's sticky cheeks. Zelda squeals and buries her face in my chest. I can feel her nose pushing against my breastbone, a little rabbit trying to burrow its way to safety.

Mama grabs hold of Zelda's shoulders and tries to twist her away from me, but the harder Mama pulls, the tighter Zelda clings.

"Mama, stop!" I say, turning my back and curling myself like a shell around Zelda.

Mama stands back, throws the wet rag on the table, and puts both hands on her hips. "A six-year-old child should not make such a fuss over getting her face wiped." She pokes a finger at me. "You, you have made her this way. With all your spoiling and giving her everything she wants. She is a difficult child now, but wait and see what she becomes. You just wait."

Zelda lifts her head up, her lashes wet with tears. She looks at Mama, and Mama looks at her. I hold my breath, feeling like something is about to snap. No one dares to move.

Except Zelda. She's the only one brave enough. My own fierce, bad Rabbit.

She sticks her tongue out at Mama.

My body tightens. What will Mama do? I'm ready to put myself between Zelda and Mama's hands. I will fight to the death if I have to.

But all Mama does is raise her eyebrows and point a silent finger at my blouse. I look down to see an orange smear across my shirt.

"That, you can wash yourself," says Mama, and she goes back to the stove and gives the clothes another stir with the wash stick.

Chapter 11

I STOOD IN THE DOORWAY TO THE PARLOR AND watched Saulie as he slept. He had one long leg on the mattress, the foot hanging over it, and one leg trailing onto the floor. His right arm curled over and around his head. The left one was crooked, the elbow pointed and sticking out over the edge of the mattress. He looked like a broken star, something that had fallen from a great height and smashed on landing.

He had kicked all his blankets off. I walked over to the mattress and crouched down, arranging the blankets over his long body. In the leaky moonlight, I could see his face, and I thought, *He's just a little boy.* His mouth was open and he was snoring. His hair looked a jungle, as if it had never met a comb. And there was still the mark of tears on his cheeks, the grimy streaks left by the quiet crying he'd done in the dark after Mama was done with him.

Mama had beaten him but good when I brought him home at eleven o'clock. She took a broomstick to him and broke it over his back. I had never seen her that angry in my whole life. She called him a hoodlum, a wharf rat, a *goniff*. "The shame you have brought to the name of your father!" she shouted at him.

It frightened me to see her hit him like that, and

LOST

I kept thinking, *Sha, sha, you're gonna wake up Zelda.* I didn't want Zelda to see Saulie getting a beating. But Zelda never woke up. All that noise, and she never woke up.

It was terrible to watch, but it also felt right that for once Mama was the one in charge of him, instead of the other way 'round. Saulie, he could have grabbed that broomstick, snapped it in two, and walked out the door. But he didn't. He stood there and took it.

Oh, he had it coming to him, all right—running the streets like he was still a kid when he had a mama and two sisters depending on him at home. But it was hard for him, I knew, because who did he have to teach him how to be a man?

I listened to his snoring in the dark. *What will Saulie do now?* I wondered. He was either going to straighten out or run away, but which, I couldn't say. He was fourteen years old, as tall as a man— old enough to be out on his own. Would he wake up, put his clothes on, and walk out the door? Who could say?

It was getting close to midnight, and I should have been in bed. There was work tomorrow, and it had been a long day. I imagined crawling into bed, Mama on one side, me on the other, and Zelda curled up between us. I wouldn't be able to see her, because of the dark. I'd gotten used to this these last two weeks, coming home late the way I'd done. The room would be dark, and I wouldn't be able to see her.

But once I was in bed, once I pulled the covers

up close to me, once I closed my eyes and let myself exhale all the thoughts of the day, then I could feel her. Right next to me, warm and breathing and asleep. That's how I pictured her, peacefully asleep. And then I could let the day go, another day, and allow myself to drift into oblivion until a new day dawned.

Tonight, though, I couldn't let go of my thoughts. There were too many swirling inside my head to go to sleep. So I pulled a blanket out of the blanket box, opened the window, and crawled onto the fire escape.

Jimmy was already out there. I could see the glow of his cigarette on Mrs. Pelz's fire escape. A quarter moon hung in the sky, just over the roof of the tenement across from ours. He didn't even ask to come over, Jimmy. He just jumped and then he was sitting next to me on the windowsill, our backs against the closed and curtained glass of the window.

"Some night," he said, and he leaned his head against the brick and closed his eyes as if remembering everything we'd done.

At the first pawnshop, where we'd sold the earrings, we'd played the part of a bickering couple, me saying he'd sell my earrings over my dead body and Jimmy shouting that if the day had come when a husband couldn't tell his wife what to do, then he'd like to know about it, *damn it!* We'd brought the price up at least three dollars.

At the second pawnshop, I'd wept bitter tears over the hatpin, and Jimmy had wrapped his arms around me, telling the broker that he just couldn't break his wife's heart like this, not for *that* price.

So maybe Zelda isn't the only one meant for Broadway.

Later at the police station, when the officer had gone down to the holding cell to haul Saulie up and bring him back to us, Jimmy had stood right beside me, close enough so that I could feel him there, my shoulder resting against his chest.

Sitting on the fire escape, too tired to say anything, I knew that it was different between us now. He hadn't asked a single question when I'd showed him the earrings and hatpin, not even one, and that meant he trusted me. And he had waited for me outside of Harriet's apartment, as long as I had needed him to wait, and so now I trusted him.

It was different between us.

"Cold, huh?" he said, blowing out a long trail of smoke and looking up at the stars.

"You want I should get another blanket?" I asked, turning to the window. It was late March. The days were hinting at spring, but the nights fell right back into the habit of winter.

"Nah, I was just sayin'."

I looked at him, and he looked at me. It's like there'd been a curtain between us, all these years. A thin, filmy curtain where I could see him and he could see me, but everything was indistinct and smudgy around the edges. But now the curtain was lifted, ripped away by everything we'd done and said tonight. I could see the shape of his face, the depth of his eyes, the curl of his lips in a way that I never had before. I felt like I could hear the beating of his heart, could feel the blood move in his veins.

When our lips met, I was surprised by the way they moved. In all my dreamings, I had imagined a kiss to be flat. I thought that lips would meet and then press and retreat. But no, that wasn't how it was at all. His lips touched mine and started to explore. They traveled slowly, like they were looking for something, the way you would run your hands along a door to find the knob when the lights are out.

My body started to scream silently. What it was screaming for, I couldn't say, but it wanted *something* and it wanted it more than anything in the world. *What comes next?* I asked myself. Something, I knew. My body knew that *something* came next. But I was sixteen years old and didn't know what it might be.

Jimmy's lips were slipping from mine, traveling down my chin and onto the slow curve of my neck. He seemed to be drinking me in, as if he were bent over a well pulling up scoopfuls of water. I had turned to liquid, my thoughts flowing without shape. His lips kept moving, and I leaned back against the window, the way water flows against a boundary. My hands were at my sides. His hand still held the burning cigarette. There was no touching between us except for his lips on my skin.

A car on Delancey backfired, making a sound like a gunshot. We jumped apart, Jimmy dropping his cigarette. I imagined its flaming tip falling four stories, landing on a pile of trash, and lighting the whole block on fire.

For a split second we stared at each other, the moonlight spilling like bathwater all around, the cool night air soaking us.

Jimmy stood up quickly. "I beg your pardon," he said. "Oh, God. I beg your pardon." He swung his legs over the railing and jumped to his own fire escape.

I was panting, panting like I'd run thirty blocks. I couldn't seem to get a real breath into my lungs. The sound in my ears of my own blood rushing—rushing with nowhere to go—made it hard to think straight.

"Don't go!" I said. "Stay here." What was I saying? What was I suggesting? I gripped the railing and leaned toward him. There was five feet between us. Only five feet and a drop of four stories. We could reach across that gap. We could fall to our deaths.

"Essie," said Jimmy. "I'm engaged to be married."

The words crossed the gap and found their way into my ears. I could hear them, but I couldn't make sense of them. "What do you mean?" I said. I needed him to make the words clear to me.

"A girl from back home. A friend of the family's. It's been arranged."

My first thought was, *This is not happening.* But it was. He was there, and I was here. And he *wasn't* reaching for me. He could have. There was just five feet between us. If he'd wanted to, he could have stayed on this fire escape with me. I had said, "Don't go." The shame of those words flooded me.

"Do you love her?" I asked. The thought went through my head that if he said *yes*, I would throw myself over the edge of the railing. But just as quickly, I thought, *No. I can't die. Zelda needs me.*

"My parents think it's a wise decision . . ." he started to say.

I stiffened my spine. "What? Are your parents going to marry her?"

"That's not fair, Essie. You know how it is." Jimmy's parents paid for him to go to law school. They paid his rent to board with Mrs. Pelz. They bought his clothes and gave him an allowance. If it weren't for his parents, Jimmy would be selling shoes in Yonkers.

"Tell me how it is," I said, wanting to hear him say it. Wanting to hear him say that a poor Jew girl from the East Side wasn't good enough for him to bring home to his mother and father.

"My parents expect things from me," he said.

"Oh, make up your own mind, Jimmy Eagan. For once in your goddamn life!" With that, I threw open the window and fell back into my own flat, my own world, my own life.

February 26, 1911

I'm sitting by the window in the parlor, trying to finish a library book what's due tomorrow. It's the last Sunday in February. The sun is spring-weak, not even strong enough to straggle into the front room this late in the afternoon. I wish I could read on the fire escape where the light is better, but it's too cold.

I'm supposed to be getting supper ready, boiling the soup bones, peeling the onions and shredding the beets, chopping the potatoes. Mama will be home from the bakery soon, carrying a loaf of stale bread under her arm. We'll soak the old bread in the thin soup and call it an end-of-the-month meal.

Mama is going to want an answer from me for why the soup isn't ready.

But first, only to read a little more of this book.

Locked within the mind of every healthy adult, there is a layer of cognitive functioning that is both dominant and hidden. This "invisible hand" directs many of our actions, shapes most of our perceptions, and controls our emotional state.

I must be reading this wrong, I think to myself. How can this be? How can the mind work without us knowing? It's like the book is telling me that sometimes my arm moves, but I don't know that it does. Of course I know when my arm moves! I can see it. I can feel it. *My* body. *My* mind. How can it be beyond my control?

Zelda is sitting on the floor, pulling my boot off and threatening to throw it out the window. She's angry with me. After a week of bitter cold, the temperature is beginning to climb. She wants to play with her friends in the street, but I won't let her. There's been a fever going around the neighborhood, and I don't want her catching it.

"You're so mean!" Zelda complains. She slaps my boot and pulls on the lace she's unhooking.

My mind snags and I have to reread the sentence I just finished.

Indeed, most of our memories and knowledge are locked away in the hidden subconscious, while only a small amount of past experience is available to us upon recall from our conscious mind.

"Zelda, stop already with the boot," I say, yanking my foot away. "Be a good girl and go play with Miss Shpilkes."

"I don't want to be a good girl," she says. "I hate Miss Shpilkes." She crawls across the floor and grabs my foot again. "I want to go outside! I hate your stupid free will."

She's remembering the book I read last week, *Time and Free Will, an Essay on the Immediate Data of Consciousness.* It was much easier to understand that book than this one. Zelda always wants to know what I'm reading, always asks a million questions.

170

I told her that free will is a person deciding for himself how his life is going to be and doing something about it, not just sitting around waiting for God to make things better. Making decisions and making things happen is free will.

"Too bad," I say, shrugging. "When I was six, I didn't have free will neither." I turn my eyes back to the book. "I'll take you to the park later. The air there is fresh. But I won't let you go in the street with sickness all around. You'll catch your death, God forbid."

"You're a *farshtunkener*," she shouts, pulling viciously on my bootlaces.

"Oh, go turn your own head around," I say right back. "You're sending me up the wall with all your cranking."

Our subconscious mind, then, is in fact the key to our existence, the answer, in many cases, to why we suffer as we do.

"Benny is outside and Myra is outside. Even that stupid Izzy Plotzkin. They have *good* mamas. I wish I had *their* mamas, instead of stupid you!"

"Zelda, you're crazy-making. *"Hoch me a chinik!"* I snap at her. The book has got to be returned tomorrow. I've renewed it once already and I can't afford a fine. I want just one hour, just one hour to read in peace. Is this too much to ask?

Zelda's quiet then, and I can feel her fussing with my boots. Fine then, if that will keep her busy.

Only to be quiet so that I can unwrap the words and crack through to the nut of the meaning.

"Essie," says Zelda, standing up solemnly. "I'm sorry. But I must to exercise my free will."

She gives me a gentle kiss on the cheek. I can smell the lemon that I squeezed in her hair last night to give it the shine and bounce. Without turning her eyes from me, she begins to back toward the door.

"Zelda!" I warn. "You are *not* going outside!"

She gets that wild look in her eyes, the one that means that life is about to get very exciting. "I have free will!" she says, her voice rising to a shriek. "I have free will!"

"Don't you dare!"

She turns and runs for the door. Before she reaches it, I jump up from my chair, but too late I realize that she's tied my bootlaces together. I land hard on my elbows, the side of my head missing the table edge by inches as I crash. I hear the rattle of the latch and then the sound of the door slamming shut.

God in heaven! I'm going to kill that little pisser! I roll over and start to pluck at my bootlaces. She's done a royal job, and it's going to take me a good five minutes to get these knots out. I keep pulling, but it's hard to bend over to get close enough to really see how the laces are tangled. I feel like I'm just making the knots tighter, the more I work at them.

Mama is going to be home any minute. She's probably walking up our block right now. She's probably spotted Zelda and will give me such a talking-to when she gets home. *I told you to keep her in. The Aberstein girl is sick with the fever, and Mrs. Feltzer's two boys, and every one of the Kesslers, too. If she comes down with it, Essie Rosenfeld, it's on your head.*

My fault. Always my fault, everything with Zelda.

Finally, I get the last loop of the knot undone. The laces fall apart from each other, and there is that feeling of bottomless relief. *Fixed.* My boots are as light as feathers now that they're free. I stand up.

But there's a moment, a vague moment, when I stand there and look at the book that's open on the table and think, *Only another minute? Just a little minute to read more, and then I'll go chasing her through the streets and bring her back. What harm could a little minute do?*

It's then that I hear the shout of the wagon master and the clang and clatter of a horse's harness pulled up short, followed by a dull thud and a woman's scream.

Chapter 12

REGRET IS THE SCRAP HEAP OF ALL EMOTIONS.

Harriet didn't show up at work on Friday. By noon, Mrs. Gullo had filled her chair, and it was like she'd never existed at all. But at the end of the day, the new girl—I never even learned her name—got sacked. She had potato hands and couldn't sew to save her life.

I knew what I would find if I went to Harriet's apartment: emptiness filled with nothing. She was gone. In my mind's eye, I saw how it happened after I left her flat on Thursday night, the earrings and hatpin in my hand. She had packed her few clothes, unlocked the desk drawer and slipped the letters from her secret lover into her pocket, blown out the lamp, and left.

Where to? I couldn't guess. Maybe she had something else to sell, something that could buy her a train ticket to Philadelphia or Syracuse or Boston. Maybe she had walked across the river and disappeared into the wilderness of New Jersey. Maybe, in the end, she had just gone back to her family.

The one thing I was sure of, though, was that she wasn't sitting in her flat waiting to be turned in by the only person in the world she had thought of as a friend.

Regret. It's like eating glass.

I could have said, "No, Harriet. I won't tell any-one." I should have said, "Your secret's safe with me." I would have said, "Don't worry. Get some sleep. It's going to be okay," if I hadn't been half out of my mind that night.

On Saturday morning, I woke up when the world was still silent and unborn. Five a.m. and the Sabbath. The whole East Side slept.

I crept out of bed and slipped into the kitchen and into my clothes. Quickly, I peeked into the par-lor to set my mind at rest: yes, Saulie was still there. Snoring and asleep. He'd spent the whole of yester-day evening in the flat, helping Mama haul the water for the wash and even fixing the broken leg of one of the kitchen chairs. He's got good hands, Saulie, when he knows what to do with them.

I let myself out the door and made my way through streets etched by their emptiness. As I left the East Side, the day yawned and stretched, start-ing to come awake. Crossing the Bowery, I walked through Little Italy, where the Saturday morning vendors were already threading their way through the streets, fighting for the best corners. I passed Lafayette, and the morning rolled over and went back to sleep as I walked through the Cast Iron District, the thin blue light of predawn hitting the empty sweatshops and factories that lined every street. At about half past five, I finally sneaked up on Washington Square Park, coming at it secretly from the south, through narrow, tree-lined streets where everyone still slept.

I let myself into Harriet's apartment and went

175

straight to the windows, dragging open the heavy curtains, letting the light, now stronger, tumble into the room. If there were ghosts to chase away, I wanted plenty of light to do the job.

"Essie?" a voice called out from the bedroom.

"Harriet? Is that you?" I asked, astonished and not believing. I started to cross the room.

"Of course it's me," she said, irritation carrying her words like drinks served on a tray. "Who else would it be? What time is it?"

"It's early," I said, reaching the door to the dark bedroom. "Not even six." I walked to the table and felt for the box of matches, then lit the bedside lamp.

"Why do you keep breaking into my apartment?" she asked. Her head was still on her pillow, her eyes closed against the lamplight. She pulled the blanket up over her head so that only one hand and a hank of hair could be seen. "Just because there's a key out there doesn't mean—! Honestly, I never should have told you about it."

"I'm so glad to see you," I said. "I thought you were gone. Gone forever."

"Not likely," she grumbled, pulling the blanket down to her chin. "Excuse my manners. I slept poorly last night. And the night before."

"Harriet, I'm not going to turn you in. The reward money, I don't need. I was crazy the other night with worry for Saulie. That's the only reason I said what I said. I'm sorry."

She waved a hand at me, then tried to pull herself into a sitting position, giving up halfway and falling back against her pillow. "I know. You were upset. I didn't think you'd really do it. Not really."

She looked exhausted, like she hadn't slept in days.

"You missed work yesterday," I said. "How come?"

"Oh, Essie," she said. "I'm just done. I can't keep going to the factory. I can't keep trying any more. I'm done." I didn't like the sound of her voice. It was a hollow, gutted sound, like the shallow breathing of an animal who has laid down to die.

"What do you mean? Are you sick?"

She groaned and covered her face with her hands. "I can't believe you don't see. I simply can't believe." She threw back the covers and rolled over so that her feet gained the floor. "Look at me," she commanded. "Look at me!"

She stood up, wearing nothing but her white chemise.

When you know someone, know them for a long time, and then something changes about them — they lose a tooth or suddenly grow thin or turn gray, hair by hair — you notice the change because you have the picture in your head of what that person used to look like. But when you have no picture and simply meet someone for the first time — missing a tooth or thin or gray — it's just a part of them, and you never stop to think that, once, they weren't that way.

I think that's why I hadn't noticed. I didn't know how she was before.

Harriet was pregnant. Not stout. Not thick in the waist. Not heavyset. Pregnant. And even though I had no picture in my head of what she used to look like, no picture to compare, I knew that Harriet's body had changed in the way that women's bodies do when they are bringing a new life into this world. Her breasts were full and drooping. Her middle sloped away from her body. Her back swayed, and her legs were set wide apart. It was like the bones in her hips were loosening and relaxing, getting ready for the work ahead. You could see how her body was falling away from its center. Expanding. Widening. Reaching out to hold the whole world.

I didn't know what to say.

I swallowed. "There never was a husband, was there?"

"No," said Harriet, sitting next to me on the edge of the bed. "When George took me to Boston in September, he promised we'd marry. But that didn't happen. Other things happened, but not a wedding. And then he went to Italy with his parents, and I found out about . . . this. I wrote to him, but he said getting married was out of the question now. I suppose he was right."

"Do you love him?" Love—I knew from all the dime novels that the girls read aloud during the dinner break—was what changed a cheap tale like this into something beautiful, something tragic.

"No," said Harriet, flatly. "In truth, I never did. But I wanted to get married. I wanted to get out of my parents' house. I wanted a home of my own."

"So your parents don't know?"

"They know. My mother's the one who sent me away in the first place. She gave me a train ticket and a thousand dollars. She made arrangements for me to go to a home for girls in the Midwest. There are places that take care of problems like this, without anyone ever knowing. You use a false name and you stay there until the baby's born and then they find someone who wants it. And you go home like nothing ever happened. My mother wanted to keep it a secret, even from my father. She was planning to tell everyone I'd gone to take the waters in Contrexéville."

"What?"

"The waters. In France. A trip abroad. For my health. It's commonly done."

"Oh. So how did you end up here?"

"I hardly know," murmured Harriet, looking at her feet, which were yellow and dirty. "I had the money and the train ticket in my purse, and the letters from George. I went for a walk down Fifth Avenue, just to get out of the house. And I kept going until I reached the park. There was a sign in a window, an apartment to let. I thought to myself, 'I've always wanted this. Why not take it? Why not? Who would ever look for me here?' It's what my mother wanted anyway—to get rid of me."

"No, I'm sure she wants you home!" I said. How could a mother turn her back on her child?

"That simply isn't true," said Harriet. "Do you remember reading in the newspapers how my mother and my brother John went to Italy to see George?"

I nodded my head.

"Did you hear how John thrashed George in that hotel lobby?" Harriet smiled just a little, and I could tell that she enjoyed that part of the story. "And my brother forced George to give him a letter that I'd written?"

"Yes," I said. The story had been front-page news every day for months. It had been like a serialized novel. Every day, the greedy public snatched up the morning papers, eager to read the next installment.

"Well, that's when John found out. Because in that letter I told George." She looked down at her mountainous middle. "I expect John told my father. Anyway, when John came home from Italy, that's when my father started telling everyone I was dead. 'It is the silence of death,' he said. The police stopped the investigation. And that was that."

"But that doesn't mean—"

"It does. Do you have any idea the scandal that would follow if people found out that the daughter of Francis C. Arnold, the niece of Justice Rufus W. Peckham of the United States Supreme Court, was having a child out of wedlock? It would bury my family. And my parents—especially my mother— care more about the good name of our family than anything else, including me."

My head was spinning. To have a family like this, one that wouldn't stick by you in the bad times—it was hard to even imagine such a thing. There had been so many times in my life when I'd envied the rich and their society ways, but this wasn't one of them.

"It was smart of you to invent a husband," I said.

"And even smarter to kill him off," said Harriet. "It got a little ridiculous, always saying to the neighbors that Gerald was off on a business trip. Nobody travels *that* much."

"So now what will you do?"

"I have no idea," she said soberly. "I don't know anything about this, having a baby. I don't know how it happens. I don't know *when* it happens. Can you imagine? I went to college, and I don't know a thing." Panic crept into her voice. "There are no books I can read about it. I can't go to a doctor. There aren't any women I can ask. Every day, I get bigger and bigger. I can't lace up my own boots. I can't fit into my skirt. I can hardly get myself out of bed in the morning. I *can't* go to work. I can't do it. And the money's all gone. Every penny of it." Her voice cracked, and the tears came. "I have no idea what I'm going to do."

I put my arms around her and let her cry all down my shirt front.

I should have been feeling sorry for her. A pregnant girl with no husband—there's *nothing* more shameful. A girl like that—she might as well take the gas, that's what her life is worth. But I couldn't. I couldn't feel sorry or sad or even frightened. All I could think of was—*a baby.*

A baby was going to come into this world— *damp skin, sweetgrass breath, wobbling fists, penny eyes*—and I wanted it—*love love love*—I wanted to wrap my arms around that small creature, bury my nose in her neck and breathe in that wonderful smell of dried milk and new skin.

Zelda would love a little sister.

"It's going to be fine," I crooned, stroking Harriet's hair, brushing the damp curls away from her face. "Trust me. I know all about babies. It's going to be wonderful. A joy! Such a joy when babies come into the world."

Harriet quieted down. "You'll help me, then?" she asked. "You'll be here when the baby comes?"

"Of course," I said. "And Mama will help, too. And Mrs. Pelz. I know they will. We won't leave you alone! I promise. Now listen to me. You have to go to work today—"

"I can't," said Harriet.

"You *have* to. Today is payday. You worked four days already this week, and your chair is still empty. So you'll go in today and work, just this last time, and collect your week's wages. *Nobody* misses work on payday."

Harriet pushed my hands away. "I can't! Everyone will know. Look at me!"

"So what if everyone knows? You're a widow. You lost your husband in a tragic accident. Hold your head up high, Mrs. Abbott. No one knows your shame."

"I can't." She shook her head. "I can't even fit into my skirt anymore. Truly, there's nowhere to move the button and I can't get it to close."

I picked up the skirt from the back of the chair and looked at it. What she said was true; there was no more room on the waistband to hold the button. I thought for a minute. "There's time," I said. "I can borrow one of Mama's skirts. She's your height, and just as thick around the middle."

Harriet looked at me like I had gone around the bend. "Why would she lend me her skirt?" asked Harriet. "She doesn't even know me."

"She just will," I said. Mama would help me. I knew that this was true. "It will take me less than half an hour to go and come back. You comb your hair. And wash your face. I'll be back soon."

Out on the sidewalk, I checked the clock in the square: half past six. There would be time, so long as I hurried. So long as Mama didn't argue. So long as Harriet didn't change her mind in the time it took me to go and come back. I could have her dressed and ready by eight. Just in time to get to work.

Later. Later there would be time to make a new plan. For now, all I wanted was to make sure that Harriet showed up for work that day at the Triangle.

February 26, 1911

I reach the second-floor landing just as Mama rushes in the front door. Her shawl is hanging off one shoulder. Her hands are empty.

Where is her basket? I wonder.

I am running, though I don't know why. Something has happened on the street, and I need to know what it is. I don't know why.

Mama catches sight of me. "No!" she shouts, and holds up both her empty hands like I'm a freight train and she's the signalman telling me that the track is out ahead. Behind Mama, Mrs. Pelz is holding the door open for a man I don't know. He's carrying something wrapped in a horse blanket. Perhaps he's a ragpicker and this is a bundle of rags. Or maybe it's a sack of coal or a bag of flour. I don't know the man, so I don't know what he's carrying.

Mrs. Pelz looks up at me and leaves the door to take care of itself. They rush at me, the two of them, like bees swarming. They grab hold of my arms and start to drag me upstairs.

"What are you doing?" I scream. "Stop it! Stop it!" I have to get to the street. I feel a pull like the street is a magnet and my blood has turned to iron.

Mrs. Bornstein opens her door on the second floor. Mama shouts, "Help, Matta!" I am fighting like a wild animal, kicking and scratching, twisting like I will unscrew my body from my legs to get away from them. "We must get her upstairs. Help us!"

Mrs. Bornstein clamps her hands on me. She

184

lifts my legs, grabbing them around the knees so I can hardly move. I'm screaming at them, begging them to put me down. Another woman on the hall comes to help them, but I can't see who it is. Mama has me by the throat, and slowly she is cutting off my air.

We reach the top landing. "Your room, Ida!" shouts Mama. "You have your key?" In less then ten seconds, they have shoved me into Mrs. Pelz's bedroom and locked the door.

The room is pitch-black. No windows. No air-shaft. Not even a particle of light to let me know which way is up and which way is down. On my hands and knees, I feel my way to the door. I grab hold of the knob and shake it with all my strength. The door holds against me.

I pound, slapping my balled-up fists on the hard wood, banging until I can't feel my hands any-more. "Let me out!" I scream, over and over, but I can tell there's no one on the other side of the door. They have left me. They are tending to something else.

There are no windows. No light. I am locked in. The air in the room is thick and qualmy. I feel like I'm breathing in cotton, heavy wads of it sticking in my lungs. There isn't enough air. I can't breathe. If I don't get out of this locked room, I will die.

Frantically, I start to feel my way around the room. There has to be a way out. I imagine my hands brushing up against rats. Spiders. The things that come out in the dark.

No light. No air. I have to get out of this room.

I crash into Mrs. Pelz's dresser, knocking off something that lands on the floor and makes the dull thud of wood on wood. I don't stop. My hands are like cockroaches, running over the walls, trying to find a way out. They sweep against a picture and it falls to the floor, the glass smashing. It crunches under my feet, the same sound my teeth make when I'm cracking chicken bones to suck out the marrow.

I am stepping over bones. I am chewing on bones.

No light. No air. I am going to die.

I work my way around the small room, finding nothing. No way out. The only way out is through the door, and the door is locked.

I throw myself against it. My shoulder bangs, taking the force. My head ricochets against the wood. The pain is like nothing I've ever felt.

I do it again. And again.

Each time, my body feels the blow less. I am going numb. From my head to my feet, I am losing the ability to feel.

The dark of the room is so deep that I can't see any part of myself. My foot at the end of my leg. My hand held up in front of my face. Dullness creeps over me. I think to myself, *I am turning invisible. No body. No feeling. Invisible.*

I throw myself against the door over and over until I feel nothing. A buzzing fills my brain and my invisible legs fold under me and I sink to the floor, a crumpled bundle of rags against the door. The buzzing is peaceful. It feels good to be settled here, neatly bundled up, tucked in on myself, invisible and numb, surrounded by quiet nothing. I can feel myself crawling into myself, crawling deeper and deeper, the way a mole seeks underground, the way a mouse creeps into the walls, the way a spider finds a crack and hides far away from the light. I am going in, going under, hiding myself away from myself, protecting.

There is no room. There is no locked door. There is no Mama or Mrs. Pelz or strange man carrying a bundle of rags. I don't need light. I don't need air. I don't need food or water. I have everything I need, deep within myself, and this is where I'll stay until it's safe to come out.

In the dark, against the door, I rock myself. Back and forth.

Over and over, I say the words, *This is not happening. This is not happening. This is not happening.*

Chapter 13

"WHY YOU ARE HOME?" MAMA ASKED, SURPRISED to see me walking in the door at seven o'clock on a work morning.

"I have a favor, please, to ask," I said. "Your other skirt, can I borrow?"

"For what?" asked Mama. She was sitting at the kitchen table, sewing up a tear in one of Saulie's shirts. "Your skirt, it looks fine."

"Not for me. There's a girl, a friend of mine from the shop. She ruined her skirt in the laundry, and she has just one. Your skirt will fit her. Can I borrow?"

"What girl? Do I know this girl?"

"You don't know. She's a friend. From the shop. Mama, she has to get to work on time. Yes or no?"

"Why should I borrow to some girl what I don't even know? Who is she to me? Tell me her name."

"Her name is Harriet. She doesn't live in the neighborhood. Just tell me if you're gonna let me take the skirt, or I'll go next door and ask to Mrs. Pelz."

"Jimmy moved out," said Mama, not looking up from her stitching. "You know about that?"

My heart squeezed, and the blood in my veins froze up, like one of those once-in-a-century winters when the East River freezes over. "Why would

I know about that?" I said, icily.

She didn't say anything and I didn't say anything, and then I asked again, "Mama, the skirt?"

Mama stood up. "You can take, but not the one in there." She started to walk toward the bedroom, unbuttoning her waistband as she went. "My other skirt is more new. This one, she can wear. I'm going to let a girl what I don't even know wear my best skirt? I don't think so."

She handed me the skirt and reached for her second one that she kept folded in her dresser drawer. "Brush it good," she said, pointing to the clothes brush on top of the dresser.

"Mama," I complained. "She don't care about a little dirt."

"*I* care," said Mama. "Brush it good."

I took the stiff wire brush to the hem of the skirt and brushed out the dust and dirt. Mama finished getting dressed and then turned to me. "Now, I want to say something to you."

I shook my head. "I don't have time, Mama. I gotta get to work."

"Sit down," she said.

I sat on the edge of the bed, the skirt folded neatly over my arm. Outside, a bell rang the quarter hour. It was seven fifteen. If I hurried. If Mama didn't talk too long. If the skirt fit Harriet just right.

You can't be late to the Triangle.

"For what I did, I'm sorry," said Mama. "I meant to protect you. I didn't want you seeing. But it was wrong. I shouldn't'a locked you up like that.

I'm sorry for it."

Mama apologizing? In all my life, I'd never heard her say she was sorry. Locking me up? I almost remembered that. Or was it from a dream? I touched my finger to the bruise on my forehead. It was long faded, almost gone.

Mama folded her arms and looked at me steady. "Mrs. Pelz says you hit your head and that's why you don't believe that Zelda's gone. She says you knocked loose your brain in that room." She was going to talk herself out to me — I could tell by the way she pushed her jaw forward. I didn't want to hear. This was craziness, what she was saying. "When they carried you out, there was blood and broken glass everywhere. The doctor, he looked at you. He said you were okay, that you just needed to rest through the night."

"I'm fine, Mama," I said. "I don't know what you're talking about, but I have to go to work now."

"No. No," she said, pressing me back down onto the bed. "Do you remember? The room?"

There was a trick to this, but I didn't know what it was. Mama was trying to trick me into something. Into saying something. Or seeing something. I pulled my arms and legs in close to me. I turned myself inward. I shook my head, barely able to get the words out. "Why would you lock me in a room?"

"Because I didn't want you to see her like that! Not like that! Not to remember her that way. Not to have the nightmares! No!"

Her words didn't make sense. There was a trick here. I pulled in more and started to close the edges of myself, sealing myself in. "Who?" I asked. "Who are you talking about?"

"Zelda. I didn't want you to see Zelda."

Ah! I *knew* Mama was up to something. I knew it. *She* was the one keeping Zelda from me. She was the one always getting between us. It was all her fault.

"Why do you hate her so much?" I shouted.

"I don't! I could never!"

"You do! You've always hated her, since the day she was born. She's always been a trouble to you. Another mouth to feed. A reminder that Papa is gone and *never coming back.*"

"You shut your mouth!" she said, slapping me with the back of her hand. "Don't you talk about your father, not like that!"

But I wouldn't stop. I stood up, towering over her. "It's true. You wished she would have died on the day she was born, and you've wished it every day since then, and that's why you say these things about her. These awful things what aren't true. You wanted her dead and now you want me to believe she is. What have you done with her?"

"Essie, listen to me." She took hold of my arms. "Only to listen. You have to believe in what is true. You have to come back from this craziness. I won't let you. I won't let you be crazy."

Mama is a powerful woman, strong arms, strong back. It's what would have caught the eye of a husband in the Old Country. But Papa, here in

America, he fell in love with her because of her laugh. That's what he always said. "I fell in love with your mama because of the way she laughs." I couldn't remember the last time I'd heard Mama laugh.

Mama held tight to me. I felt like I couldn't move. She had me pinned to the spot, and I couldn't move. "I'm not crazy," I said.

"Only to listen! You are strong enough to hear this. It's my fault. I should have let you see her that day."

"Why didn't you? Why did you lock me in that room? Why couldn't I see Zelda?"

"Because of her face," said Mama. "The horses, they trampled her. She got caught under the horses. Her face, it was broken, all smashed in. There was nothing there when they pulled her out. I didn't want you to see. I didn't want you to remember her like that."

I broke free from her grip. I spat on the floor. "Liar." Then I pushed Mama out of the way and ran out of the flat.

February 27, 1911

SUCH A HEADACHE. IT TAKES MY BREATH AWAY.

I sit on the edge of the bed and try to find the strength to stand. I feel as though someone has put my head in a pipe wrench and is slowly tightening the screw. Is it time for my monthly? I try to count the weeks on my fingers, but I'm too tired to lift my hand.

Mama is still asleep. I can't see her; the room is too dark. But I hear her breathing on the far side of the bed. I wonder why she isn't at the bakery already. She should have been at work two hours now.

Zelda is asleep, too. No sound at all from her, but I know she's there, curled in the curved hollow of the space between Mama and me. I've slept next to her every night for six years, and I know what it is to have her beside me. Without even touching her, I can feel her warmth, her dreamings, the humming vibration of her sleep. She's so much a part of me that I don't need to see her or touch her to know that she is safe and well beside me. I can feel it in my bones. She is well.

I push myself to my feet and totter into the kitchen. I need coffee, but it's the end of the month and all we have is chicory. I decide to take a penny from the cracker tin and buy a cup on the street. I'm hoping this will help to glue my head back onto my shoulders and get me through the morning.

In the end, I slip three pennies into my pocket, not having the strength to bundle up a dinner in my string bag. I'll buy a biscuit at the noon hour from the corner pushcart. Mama will scream herself blue in the face when she sees the money is gone and the rent due in two days, but I'll figure some way to fix it. I can always fix things.

In the dark I feel for my skirt hanging over the back of a chair, but I can't find my blouse and so I light a lamp. My blouse is draped over the slop sink, and when I pick it up I see that someone tried to wash a stain out of it last night. There's a faint, dull-brown spot on the front and another on the sleeve.

Ach! Who could have been so clumsy? Immediately I blame Saulie for spilling something on my blouse after I went to bed. Mama must have tried to ready it for the morning, but the blouse will need ironing and I haven't got time to light the fire and heat the irons before going to work. I'll have to wear my second blouse to work today.

I steal back into the bedroom and feel my way to the dresser, which is on Mama's side of the bed. Quietly, I pick up the hairbrush and begin to brush out my hair. Every time the brush touches my head, it's like a hammer slamming down. I'm nearly crying by the time I'm done. Slowly I pin up my hair in the dark. I'm used to doing this without being able to see myself. There hasn't been a mirror in the flat since Papa died.

When the last pin is in, I pat my head, feeling for stray hairs. On one side the hair feels stiff, and I gently poke with my fingers. There's something dried there, above my ear. It flakes away when I touch it, but in the dark I can't tell what it is.

I catch up a wisp of hair that hangs in front of my eyes, and my fingers feel a tender spot on my forehead near the hairline above my right eye. When I press it with my finger it broadcasts an empty, lonely ache through my skull and down my spine.

I press again.

I almost like the feeling.

Mama moans in her sleep. I have to finish dressing. I can't be late for work. I ease open the middle drawer and feel my way through the pile of clothes. I know exactly what my blouse feels like—the roughness, the thickness of the cloth, the stitching of the seams. In the deep black of the room, I slip the blouse out and slide the drawer closed.

Mama wakes up. Slowly at first, and then she is sitting up and fully alert. "Essie?" she asks. Why is her voice edged with fear?

"*Sha*, Mama, it's just me," I say, slipping my arms through the sleeves of my blouse. "Go back to sleep." I think on what Mama used to say when we were little, *Go back to the happiness of dreams.*

"Essie, are you all right?" she asks.

"Fine, Mama, I'm fine. Only don't talk so loud. You'll wake up Zelda."

I walk back out to the kitchen, buttoning up my blouse as I go. My fingers are stiff and swollen. My head is still pounding. It feels like it weighs as much as a potato basket. I sit down to lace up my boots and almost think I will faint from leaning over.

Mama appears in the doorway. "Not to go to work today, Essie," she says quietly.

I start to laugh, but the pain shoots into my head and stops me short. "*Pffff*. Mrs. Gullo! She would like that," I say. "It's Monday, Mama, and Monday is a work day."

I take my hat down from the peg and put it on my head. The brim of the hat presses against the tender spot and sends a shivering ache down my back. In one swift movement, I thread the hatpin through the crown, checking with my hands to make sure I've pinned it on straight. A hat worn crooked, even a good one, looks cheap. I always wish I could teach the young girls: *Take the time to pin your hat on straight. It makes all the difference in the world.*

I'm reaching for my shawl when Mama says, "Zelda isn't asleep in the bedroom."

I take the shawl and rope it over my shoulders. I have everything I need. I'm ready to go. "Then she must be hiding. That's our game. She likes to hide."

Mama starts to talk, but I don't let her. I won't listen to what she has to say. I talk right over her, raising up my voice so that it floods out her words, washes them away, washes them into the gutter and carries them down the sewer.

"Mama, she's hiding! Stop making such a *tsimmes*. She'll come out when she's ready. It's our game. *Our* game. You don't understand how we play. Zelda is fine."

I walk out of the flat, half expecting Zelda to

pop out at me from the top of the stairs. There are so many places she likes to hide. Every time we play, she finds a new spot. I could search for a week and still not find her, if she made up her mind to stay hidden from me.

Once on the street, I take the shortest route out of the neighborhood, glancing just once over my shoulder to see if Zelda is waving to me from our fire escape. *I expect she'll be there when I get home,* I say to myself, and keep on going.

It's a Monday. An ordinary Monday. A Monday like any other, and I can't be late for work.

Chapter 14

THE CLOSING BELL RANG AND THE POWER WENT dead. I stood and stretched, my back aching from the long day.

What a day it had been.

Working in a shop, you have to keep your mind on your machine and the work in front of you. If you daydream, you'll end up with your hand stitched to a waist.

But that day, my thoughts were like ants on a hill, running crazy. I kept thinking about Harriet leaving her family. About everything she'd lost — her money and her brother and her home and even her name. And all that losing made me think of Jimmy. Jimmy was gone, probably forever. I would never see him again or hear his voice or touch his hand. We would never — not ever — sit on the fire escape together, talking with Zelda curled between us. And that thought brought me around to the tea party tomorrow, and the invitation still in my skirt pocket, and then came the dark and lonely feeling creeping around the edges of all my thoughts like a cat on its haunches, tense, waiting to pounce.

And, just to add to the craziness I was feeling, one sparkling and bright thought kept darting in and out of all the heavy ones: Harriet was going to have a baby. A baby! *Like an angel from heaven, this child is to me.* I thought of delicate fingers that wave at nothing, legs curled like little worms, the gurgling and cooing, and the eyes that drink you in. A baby! The thought of it made me want to lift up my skirts and dance.

There was so much to do! At the noon break, Harriet and I had decided that I'd go home after work and pick up my sewing things, then meet her back at her apartment. First things first, she needed a skirt she could wear. Mama would want hers back; that was only fair. But there would be time after work to find a couple of good ready-wears on the street, and at a price she could afford. Thank God Mama had taught me how to haggle with the peddlers.

I looked across the table. Harriet was still working a seam. The power was gone from her machine, but she was turning the flywheel by hand and stitching, one slow stitch at a time.

"Day's done!" I shouted over the noise of all the girls who were talking, talking, talking.

She kept at it. "I want to finish," she called back, and then she looked at me. "My last one. I want to finish it."

I could understand that. It was frustrating when you had just a few inches left of a seam, so little to do to make the shirt whole, complete. And the power died and you were left hanging there, the thing undone. I could understand her wanting to walk out of the Triangle for the last time with that waist in her basket.

"You have your wages?" I asked. She patted

her blouse to show me that she had her money safely tucked away, but didn't take her eyes off the seam. It was hard work turning the flywheel and keeping the stitches straight.

Freyda turned around and smiled at me. Closing time! Payday! Tomorrow, a day off from work! Everywhere, you could hear girls talking about their weekend plans, talking about how they would spend their wages, talking and talking. Two hundred and forty girls humming with excitement. I smiled back at Freyda. She jutted her thumb at Harriet. "What's with?"

"She wants to finish the seam," I said.

"Harriet, you work too hard!" said Freyda. "It's the weekend. Time to stop, already!"

Harriet waved her flywheel hand at Freyda, but kept right at it. Freyda and I looked at each other and shrugged.

"G'night, Harriet," called Freyda. "See you on Monday!"

"Goodnight," said Harriet, looking up for just a split second to smile at Freyda and me before turning back to her machine.

"I'm going home," I said to Freyda. "You want we should walk together?"

Freyda smiled and nodded. "Only I've got to get my hat and shawl from the coatroom. Maybe you could wait on the street?"

"*Eh*, I'll come with," I said.

Freyda and I were halfway to the coatroom, the girls moving like cattle through a gate, when the air split apart with the sound of an explosion. I turned around to see; we all did. A window, one of the tall ones that went from floor to ceiling and looked out over Washington Place, had shattered.

Before I could even think on this, another window exploded. Shards of glass fired into the shop, slicing the faces of the girls who were closest. Then another window exploded, and another. A girl screamed, "Fire!" and I saw that it was true. Fire was climbing up the outside of the building and reaching through the broken windows onto the shop floor.

Girls panicked. Screams filled the air. Suddenly, Freyda's body slammed into mine as she was pushed backward. The girls in front of her had turned around and were rushing for the staircase behind us. I was pushed down, but caught myself on the edge of a table. Freyda fell on top of me and then rolled off and onto the ground, and the girls started to step on her.

"Girls, please!" screamed Freyda. "You're killing me!" But the girls weren't girls anymore; they were a stampeding herd. I yanked myself up and began to punch and kick at the girls to keep them off of Freyda. Keeping one arm stiff in front of me, I reached with the other and pulled her to her feet. Her nose was bleeding and she hunched forward, one hand pressing against her ribs. All the time, I could hear the strange sound: the loud *pop* followed by the shattering of glass. All the windows were exploding, and the hungry fire licked its way in.

Everything was burning. Scraps of fabric went

up like paper. Cups of oil for greasing the machines. Wooden chairs. Baskets and clothing and girls.

I grabbed Freyda's hand and started to pull her toward the exit. We weren't so very far, but other girls had pushed in front of us and now there was a knot of screaming girls all trying to push through the narrow door. They couldn't fit, not all at once. They had clogged the exit and were tearing at each other and screaming, ripping each others' hair and clothes. Some of the girls had fainted dead away, falling to the ground, and the other girls were trampling over them.

Smoke poured out of the stairwell, filling the air, making it hard to breathe. I felt as though a cord was wrapped around my throat, pulling tighter and tighter. The heat had turned solid, a thing to push against. Moving through it was like dragging through waist-high mud.

Freyda and I were now in the center of a clot of girls, still too far from the exit to get through. Suddenly, there was a tremendous explosion. A fireball bloomed in front of us and rolled out of the stairway, steamrolling the girls who were closest. The barrel of machine oil that was stored in the vestibule next to the stairs had exploded. The girl who had been near the doorway staggered back and fell, the skin burned off her face, her clothes turned to black ash. I could see the white bones of her cheek poking through.

This is not happening, I said to myself. *This is not happening.*

The stairway was filled with flames. There was no way to get through.

Freyda was still behind me. I turned to her. There was blood trickling down the side of her head. She didn't seem to know where she was or what was happening. I shouted, "C'mon!" and began to push her up the aisle. Half of her hair had come undone. It was hanging, a lazy snake that reached to her waist.

Behind me, I heard a sharp scream and then, "Essie!" I turned and saw that it was Yetta Goldstein. Her skirt had caught on fire and she was twisting, first right and then left, trying to get away from herself. It was like watching a dog trying to catch its own tail.

I let go of Freyda and started to slap at Yetta's skirt, as if I could punish the fire into obeying me. My own skirt caught on fire. It felt like some strange animal was climbing up my body. Some evil, scratching cat that breathed fire as it raced up my skirt. The more I slapped at it, the faster it climbed.

Crazy, I looked around for a fire bucket. There was one nailed to a pillar, just three feet down the aisle. I grabbed it—but the bucket was empty, bone dry. I ran down the aisle to the next one, and that bucket was empty, too. The fire was at my waist. It circled me like a hoop.

From behind me I felt a stab and then a pull and heard tearing. I thought, *Gott im himmel, the fire has grown teeth.* But when I turned around, there was Freyda, a pair of scissors in her hand. She was cutting my skirt off me, tearing it and slashing it to ribbons. When I was free, we turned and ran back up the aisle. There was Yetta, not moving—lying on the floor, wrapped in a cocoon of flames.

This is not happening.

Freyda took a step back and sat heavily on one of the tables. Her arms hung like deadweights at her side, and her face looked like she was sleeping with her eyes open.

A thought screamed through my brain. *Harriet!* Where was she? I scrambled onto a table and stood up, but the choking smoke forced me to my knees. Coughing like I would bring up my own lungs, I couldn't even call out her name. I covered my mouth with my sleeve and tried to stand again.

I saw her through the haze. She was sitting in her chair at her sewing machine. One hand was on the flywheel; the other was still on the waist, holding it taut, ready to feed it forward to take the next stitch. She was frozen, looking at the wall of fire in front of her. The cup of grease on the table beside her was burning. Flames shot three feet into the air, just inches from her machine. All around her, baskets of waists were burning and the fire from the window was licking her hair.

I watched.

Her clothes caught quickly, making a column of the flames. Her hair curled and blew upward, carried by the updraft. The skin on her face blackened. Her eyes became huge—they looked like they would swallow her whole face.

She never moved.

I tried to call out, *"Harriet,"* but the word was caught in my throat, stuffed down inside of me by the choking fist of the smoke. I tried and tried again, as if my calling her name could save her, as if that name could rain down on her—cool, welcome water—quenching the fire that circled her and swallowed her. I reached deep inside of me for air that wasn't there and tried to call it up, a long-forgotten magic trick. *Harriet.* But nothing came.

Inside my head, I whispered, *Dorothy.*

I felt a hook rip through me, slashing a great hole through my center. The hole was black and bottomless, and I felt myself falling forward into it, falling into myself, where I would disappear and be lost forever.

Beside me, Freyda moaned. I fell down from the table and took her hand.

Freyda. *Here, not gone.*

Holding tight to her, I pushed into the crush of girls, all fighting to get to the back stairs and the two elevators near the coatroom. A few broke out of the knot and began to run madly down one of the sewing aisles. Girls behind me pushed to follow them, and Freyda and I were carried down the aisle.

"No! Not this way!" I shouted. "Girls! Only think! There's no way out here!"

But the girls were beyond listening. One had broken from the pack and the others were following her, down the aisle to the row of blown-out windows. Glass crunched under my feet. It was all I could do to keep from stumbling. We were car-

ried along on the tide of girls desperate to find a
way out of the fire.

The girl who had broken away first—it was
Albina Caruso, a button-setter who had gotten
engaged just last week—climbed up onto the windowsill at the end of the aisle. Without looking
back, she stepped off the sill. I watched as she
walked out into the air and disappeared.

Freyda screamed and squeezed my hand 'til I
thought it would break. I couldn't move.

Then another girl—it was Ida from our row—
climbed onto the sill, and two more with her.
Freyda screamed, "Ida! Don't jump!" but the
sound was like a whisper in a hurricane. All three
girls held hands, and then they stepped off the windowsill.

Anna Altman was next. She stepped onto the
windowsill. She opened the small brown envelope
that held her week's wages and let the bills flutter
into the air. They looked like birds taking wing, so
delicate and light. Then she tossed the coins ahead
of her and walked into the air.

This was madness. There had to be a way out.
Freyda was coughing so hard, she was bent at the
waist. The girls behind us were pushing us down
the aisle toward the windows. I yanked on Freyda's
hand. "This way," I shouted, and pulled her up
onto the sewing table, out of the rushing river of
girls desperate to jump.

I could just see through the smoke and across
the shop. The back staircase was blocked, a wall of
girls pressed up against the locked door. Mrs.

Gullo was there, desperately trying to calm the girls, but no one was listening to her. We had to get to the elevators. They were the only way out.

I turned to tell Freyda my plan: that we had to jump from table to table to get across the shop and to the elevators. She didn't seem to understand me. She didn't seem to understand that we had to go anywhere. I was facing her, holding her by the shoulders, shaking her to make her understand. She put her hand to her ribs. She was hurt. The air was getting thicker. Soon we wouldn't be able to breathe.

I took Freyda by the hand, and together we jumped to the next table and then the next and the next. Each table was a minefield with exploding cups of grease shooting flames into the air. Freyda landed wrong, coming down hard with her left foot half off the table. She fell forward and couldn't get back up on her feet. We had to crawl across the tables, threading our way through the sewing machines, dodging the pools of fire. Halfway across the room, I could feel my hair beginning to burn. I smacked at it, hitting myself in the head until I thought I would go unconscious.

When we reached the pack of girls at the elevator, I screamed, "Are they running?"

"Yes!" shouted one of the Italian girls at the back of the knot. "But they don't stop. They go up to the tenth. They don't stop here! Jesus, our God! Don't let us burn!" The tenth floor was where the bosses worked. They kept accounts up there, ran payroll, made sales. I had never been on the tenth floor.

The girls banged on the closed elevator gate

and pushed the call button over and over. All of a sudden, a girl near the front shrieked, "It's stopping! It's stopping!" The crowd pushed forward, and when the door to one elevator cage opened, the girls closest were pushed to the ground and others trampled over them to get in.

I could hear Joseph, the elevator boy, shouting, "Too many! Too many! I gotta close the door. I'll come back!" I watched as the elevator door closed, crushing fingers that reached forward to pry it open. And then it was gone.

A wail, like nothing I had ever heard in my life, rose up. Part scream, part song, it filled my ears until I thought I would drown in it.

A moment later, the door to the other elevator opened. Gaspar pressed himself against the cage, trying to make as much room as possible for the girls to climb on. The crowd trampled and clawed, each girl fighting her way into the elevator that was no bigger than a small closet. As the cage door to the elevator began to close, one girl dived headfirst onto the heads of the girls in the elevator. I could see her feet sticking straight out into the elevator shaft as the elevator disappeared down, down.

Freyda and I had pushed our way to the middle of the pack. Behind me, the girls at the back of the crowd were starting to catch fire. I heard their shrieks as their dresses caught. It was a different scream from the screams of the frightened girls at the front. It sounded like something being ripped in two.

The girls at the back pressed harder and harder

into us. They were being eaten by fire and had nowhere to go. One girl tried to climb up and over us, like we were a bridge that she could cross. But she fell into the pack and got trampled.

Suddenly, I heard a voice from the front shout, "I see the elevator. It's coming." But then, immediately, a scream of grief. "The tracks, they are twisted. It cannot rise. It's going down! It's going down!" The girls began to shriek even more than before. One elevator was gone. Only one remained.

I had been inching my way forward, pushing Freyda in front of me. We were now near the front of the crowd, with a layer of girls four deep between us and the elevator shaft. Freyda's face was pressed into the back of the girl in front of her. She twisted her head, trying to tilt it up, trying to find air. "I can't breathe," she gasped. "Oh, God, help me!" I shoved my hands under her arms and tried to lift her higher, but it was impossible to raise her with no room to move.

"It's coming," shouted one of the girls in front. "The other elevator's coming."

I thought my life would be squeezed out of me. When the doors opened, the push forward was like an explosion, sudden and violent. Girls screamed in pain as they were stomped on, shoved, slammed against the wall, scraped against the grating. I heard someone begging for mercy, "Please! No! Please!" It was as if every one of us knew that this was the last time the elevator would reach the ninth floor. I shoved Freyda from behind, pushing her toward the elevator. I pushed so hard, I thought I would break her in two.

The elevator doors began to close, scraping the backs of my hands. There was a loud *click* as the catch hooked.

Freyda was on the elevator. I was not.

Freyda screamed, "Essie! Essie!" Frantic, she tried to twist herself around. One of her hands grabbed hold of the grate and clawed at it.

The elevator started to go down, opening up the great hole of the elevator shaft in front of me. I stood there, on the edge of the shaft, watching the elevator grow smaller and smaller. The girls behind me shrieked and moaned and wept and prayed, pushing against me. I had to press with all my strength against the frame of the shaft to keep from falling in.

I listened as Freyda screamed my name, over and over. "Essie! Essie!"

Essie.

I peeled that name off of me.

Harriet was dead. I had seen her die. I had *seen*.

How easily it all comes unraveled. What a simple trick it is to peel the soul away from the flesh.

Harriet.

Floating in my brain was another name, weaving itself in and out of what I had just seen and what I now knew.

Zelda.

My fierce, bad Rabbit. My own good luck. My child.

I wanted to die.

The black, bottomless hole that had ripped

inside me melted into the dark hole of the elevator shaft, until it was all one thing. Me and the pain and the loss and the screams and the smoke and the smell and the darkness of that tunnel—there was no space between them, no boundaries to honor, no fences to cross, no obligations to hold me. And so I let go, and I fell.

Chapter 15

I OPENED MY EYES. THE SKY WAS GRAY AND rolling. A storm, perhaps. I was lying on the side-walk. *How strange*, I thought, *to be lying here on the sidewalk in the middle of the day. I wonder if anyone will notice.*

But all around me, people were running and shouting and no one noticed me at all. I remember thinking that I had crossed over something, some kind of wall or fence that separated me from every-one else. I seemed to be divided from all the people running and screaming and shouting out names and orders and curses.

Ahh. The thought came slowly, but then I knew.

I had finally become invisible. Like I knew I would. I had disappeared, right in front of every-one's eyes.

Right on the street, in broad daylight. Imagine that. A person can just disappear.

What a magic trick, that.

I turned my head, feeling the sharp bite of the sidewalk on my scalp. What a surprise! There was a girl lying next to me. Her eyes were open and she stared up at the dark sky. It was beginning to snow, soft gray snowflakes that swirled up whenever someone rushed past us. Magical snow.

"Why are we lying down?" I asked her, but she didn't answer. She didn't even turn to look at me.

The snow was so beautiful. I thought: *She can't take her eyes off it. She's transfixed.*

So I turned my head the other way. My eyes swept across the sky, and I saw water shooting through the air in a long glittering arc, like fireworks. I kept turning my head, scraping it against the sidewalk, until I could see what was on the other side of me.

There was another girl. A little slip of a thing, so small I could have fit her in my pocket and still had room for change. Her skirt was torn. She was missing one shoe. Her small hand was curled like a kitten at her side. But she had no face. It had been smashed in.

"Oh, it's *you*," I said.

Just like Mama said. Her face, her beautiful face, gone. Her head trampled by the horses who were afraid and half out of their minds. You couldn't blame *them*. I saw her. *I finally saw her.* Just like Mama said.

"Come here," I said, trying to reach my arms across my body to gather her up. There was a sudden burning pain in my chest and I couldn't pull in a breath. My arms felt like cement, but I struggled to lift them and reach over to her. "I can fix that," I said. But I knew that I couldn't. No one on earth could fix this. It felt like there was a huge distance between us, even though I could see with my eyes that she was just inches away from me. But it felt like there was a river between us, deep and wide.

Zelda was dead. She was lost to me and never coming back. There was no use fighting anymore.

I gave in, lay down my sword.

The dark thing was there, lurking on the edges of my vision. Animal thing, it smelled my fear. I waited for the sharp claws, the bite of teeth. I waited to be ripped limb from limb.

Instead, a kiss, on my lips.

I moaned.

And then there was shouting nearby, and I heard a woman scream and a man's voice call out, "This one's alive. Over here. She's alive!" And then I stopped being invisible and there were hands on my body lifting me up, lifting me up and carrying me away from my little girl.

Chapter 16

I AM LYING IN A BED THAT IS A BOAT THAT IS A COFfin that is floating in an ocean of fire with waves of flame and ice. The ocean is as flat as glass and I am unmoving in a world that spins around me, turning and twisting on the pike of an axis that pokes straight through my ribs, that slices my trunk in half like a fish that is gutted and flayed, laid open to dry out in the sun. The world is spinning, but I have become the center of the universe, and I am still, as still as a body at rest on the bottom of the East River, as still as a cold polar star, as still as a grave. But the world around me is turning and the waves on the flaming ocean dash over the edge, splash and dash themselves over the lip of the boat, the cracked and split lip of this wooden death boat and I am washed in heat and then cold and I burn and I shake and I shiver as the fire and ice wash over me and the sound of the air torn in half fills my ears, the tearing, screaming sound of life ripped from soul, of breath torn from bone, the screaming, the screaming, and then the needle the needle and the screaming huddles in on itself and becomes its own memory and a dull buzz rises as the waves settle back into the flat, glassy sea. And the edges of everything are mossy soft and velvet like the ears of an old dog like the dusty wings of a moth and I can breathe and I open my eyes and there you are.

I can hardly speak. I choke on the words that snag in my scarred throat. "Is it you? Really?" I finally manage to say.

Your eyebrows shoot up. You flick your hands, palms to the ceiling. Without a word, you say, "So, does it look like me?"

You think my question is stupid. But I only asked because I want to hear your voice, so I ask it again. "Is it you?" My eyes burn. They want to blink, but I won't close them. I don't want to miss one second of you, not one split-infinity second of you.

You shake your head *no*, sad and serious—just like you used to do. "It's the morphine."

But I won't listen to you. You're only six, after all. What do you know?

This is bliss.

I wonder if I can touch you. The wonder becomes a hunger and the hunger blooms into starvation and I think that if I don't feel the small shell of your hand in mine, if I don't touch your river hair, if I don't smell your little-girl breath on my face, I will curve myself into a ball and die.

But I'm afraid that if I try to get too close, you'll disappear. Fly away? Go up in smoke? Jump from the window? Tie my laces into knots and run out the door? I haven't got the guts to risk it.

So I think: I'll creep up on you, inch by inch, so slow you won't even notice. You've moved from one side of the bed to the other, closer to the window now, which makes my heart race. I don't like you close to the window. The light through the clean glass cuts shadows across your face, planes of bright and dark that make you look prismatic. I shrug my shoulders, dig my elbows into the coffin-bed, and try to ease myself up. I try so hard to make this movement small, so small, no more than a light breeze blowing through the room. But my muscles are weak. My legs jerk under the sheet, and you make the move of a startled rabbit, ready to bolt.

And then there are The Hands on me, invisible hands and a buzzing in my ear that rises and falls the way words do, only I can't make out the words. But The Hands, The Hands I know. I have known them since the day I was born. They press me back into the coffin. They work the edges of me, kneading and pressing, the way I have watched them work a loaf of bread a hundred times — straightening and tucking the sheets, curling back a strand of hair from my face, pressing a towel to my forehead, folding my hands over themselves, and curving the unbandaged tips of my fingers into a cup. The Hands work the edges of me, my center wrecked beyond reclaim.

And there is singing now, or humming, maybe. I can't make out the words but know them the way I know my name and yours and the names of those who came before. *Esther means* star, *and Papa said that's why I turned out so beautiful*... It's how the story goes, and I know it, the way you know your nursery rhymes and I know the song that Mama is now humming by the side of my bed.

In the room of the temple,
In a cozy corner,
There sits a widow all alone.

"But Mama," I whisper. "I'm not beautiful any-more."

"Stop it," you say. You point a finger at my bed. "You're making Mama cry."

"Not so close to the window," I whimper, think-ing, *Who are you to boss me around?* "It makes me nervous."

You move away from the window and to the foot of my bed. I sink into the pillows, and The Hands disappear, slipping back below the surface of the water.

There's a silence between us, and you start to fade a little, as if it's just our talk that's keeping you here, so I scramble to string together some words and all I can come up with is, "So, then, you're an angel?"

You purse your lips and look at me out of the sides of your gorgeous eyes. "Wasn't I always?"

And I laugh and say, "No! You were a fierce, bad Rabbit!" And then you jump down on all fours and start to hop around the floor, snarling and slashing your Rabbit paws at unseen enemies, and I laugh so hard and suddenly that The Hands are on me again, pressing, pressing, pressing.

You stand up and stamp your booted foot. "Don't laugh, either," you scold. "It upsets her. She needs a rest, you know, so quit with the crying, would ya?"

I shake my head, *no*. "You don't get to say." I make it clear. "You got no right, coming back and telling me this or that. *You're* the one who left."

"*Oy gevalt*, hand me a hankie, why don't you? So I died. It happens. What? Are you going to wring my neck for it?" You're playing with the hem of your dress. There's a thread hanging down and you're trying to break it with your fingers.

This child! The words explode out of me. "You. *You* went out in the street. I told you not to. I *told* you!" I imagine leaping off the bed and grabbing you by the shoulders and shaking you—shaking you until you understand *what you have done*.

"Me?" you say. "Is this a joke you're telling me? I'm six years old. You could have followed me. You could have dragged me back inside. Please! You're making me laugh with this story you're telling."

"You tied my boots together! In knots. I practically knocked myself out on the table!"

"*Oy*, the knots! You had them undone in seconds. And your head was fine, not even a bump. It was the book. Do you remember the book?"

I remember the book. It had pulled at me. It had promised me the world, promised to explain the how and the why of my life. It had seemed so important at the time.

You nod your head, watching me remember. "You wanted to read it. You wanted to read that book more than you wanted to take care of me. You had free will, Essie, and you chose the book."

I want to scream—not at you, but at that book and the world and myself and the past that I can't change. I want to scream so loud that I explode the past. Is that possible? To create a thing—a noise, a pain, a fire—so enormous that it can destroy the past? I want to try, and so I close my eyes and open my mouth and fill my lungs—but all that leaks out is a thin whimper, high-pitched and weak, more injured than injuring.

How pathetic.

The whimper calls forth The Hands. They pet the crown of my skull. They circle over my forehead. They stroke my lips to quiet them.

I must be quiet for Mama. She has suffered enough.

But there *is* a sound, not a scream, not a whimper, and I open my eyes again, and it is singing, and it is coming from you. Oh! You are singing! And oh, it is so beautiful. A song without words, the notes rising and falling like a butterfly in flight. You were always the musical one in the family.

I want the song never to end, because it tells me something, even without words: I am forgiven—by you, by God, by myself. The anger is emptied out of me, and the shame and the regret. And all I am left with is a longing, a longing to be with you forever.

When you finish, I ask, "Who taught you that song?"

You say, "God," and shrug like it's not much that He has been teaching you songs, that you know whole songs I've never even heard before. I was your world, and now you know such songs as these?

And I say, "I am ready to go to God." I take a deep breath in and then let it out. Oh, the relief of it. I can be with you. I don't have to wait. I don't have to suffer anymore.

But you say, "No. You had your chance. And you threw it away."

"When? When did I have the chance?" *How dare you say such a thing?*

You are tugging at your sash. The bow has worked its way to the side, and you are trying to muscle it back into place. You don't even look up at me. "When you jumped. When you jumped into the elevator shaft—that was your chance. We could have been together, but no. You grabbed hold of the cable. You could have let yourself fall down the shaft, but you didn't. You reached out and grabbed the elevator cable. You saved yourself. *You* didn't die."

"I didn't mean to! It was a mistake! I never meant to do it!" The walls of my chest are splitting in two, splitting where the cable sliced open my shirt, sliced open my skin, and cut me all the way to the bone. I remember holding on desperately to the cable as I slid down the elevator shaft, down past the eighth floor, the seventh floor, the sixth floor, the fifth floor, the fourth floor, the third floor—where I passed out and landed on top of the elevator cage and then was carried out and laid on the sidewalk, left for dead.

You shrug as if to say, *What's done is done.*

"It isn't fair," I say, knowing that fairness has nothing to do with it. We make choices. Sometimes over years, sometimes in a split second.

I take in a long breath. "Zelda," I say. I hadn't let myself say your name before. I'd been holding it in, holding it in all this time, but now it comes out like the tendril of smoke that rises when you blow out a candle. I look at you for one long, last, loving second. "You're not really here, are you?"

"No," you say, wrinkling your nose. "I told you from the beginning. It's just the morphine."

I nod my head. I knew. I really knew all along. From the moment you moved away from the window when I asked you to. My Zelda would never have done that. You never obeyed me, my own fierce, bad Rabbit.

"Maybe I could stay like this forever," I say, thinking that wouldn't be so bad. To lie in this coffin-bed and slip in and out of morphine dreams and see you and listen to you and maybe, who knows, maybe someday I could reach out and touch you.

"No," you say. "You can't. You're going to get better. You're going to live."

"Do I have to?" I am suddenly so tired, the thought of taking in even one more breath feels beyond my strength.

"Yes."

"Why?" I'm thinking of my free will, and I'm thinking of choosing not to breathe anymore.

You are flouncing your skirts around you and doing a little waltz-curtsy to the left and the right, getting ready for your big exit. "Because you're young and you're strong and you have the instinct to grab hold of a cable what's in front of you. That's why." Then you stop with the flouncing but still hold tight to your skirts and you look right at me. "And because Mama needs you to live." You pick up your skirts and hold them out—a pretty pose— and the end has come.

"Just, could you please?" I am afraid to ask. "Please, could I hold you one more time?"

You drop your skirts and grin and run at me, run like a freight train on a straightaway, right at me, as if you will knock me flat with your love for me. And I throw open my arms and can almost feel it, feel the cool mist of you as you run at me and through me and are gone.

Chapter 17

THE HAT WAS FINISHED. IT HAD TAKEN ME THREE nights. Three nights of staying late after closing the shop. Three nights of extra work after filling the day's orders. Three nights of cutting and shaping and sewing and ripping and re-sewing and then ripping again until I knew for sure that the hat was done. Sometimes, it's hard to know with a hat.

I stuck out my thumb, the one on my crippled hand, and rested the hat on the tip. It balanced, swaying like a bell in a breeze. This was good. It's important for a hat to have balance.

I looked at the crazy pattern I had made, the strange swirl of horsehair and lacquered straw that began at the crown and spiraled out to the brim. With my good hand, I spun the hat on my thumb. The black spirals seemed to fly out from the middle. It was like a carousel at a fun park. It was like a cyclone touching ground. It was like a whirlpool in a river. It was like the end of the world, the way I remembered it.

It had come out of my mind. Out of the warm, dark, bubbling place inside my head where thoughts and memories and dreams swim together. I hadn't copied it from a Paris model. I hadn't seen it in another shop window. It had been born out of me entirely—and it was strange, twisted, hideous, and almost beautiful.

Now that it was made, I thought of putting it out with the day's trash. It was certainly a hat that would be bad for business. *Mad as a hatter*, my customers would say.

I spun the hat one more time. It was insane, the way the spirals played tricks on the eye.

I walked over to the window display and lifted up the black velvet boater with the weeping ostrich plume that I had finished just last week. That hat had already brought in six orders. It was my new best seller. I heard Mama's voice in my head, "No, no. Not to take away the good-selling hat and replace it with that crazy one. Always, the more business you want." But even with Freyda working overtime for me, I would need to hire at least one—probably two—girls before the summer season started. Business was good. I was grateful.

The hat rested beautifully on the frilled hat stand in the center of the display. Was it my imagination, or did the other hats shuffle a little off to the side? Well? Nobody likes things that are different. Didn't I get the same when people saw my scarred face, my claw hand?

I looked up and saw myself reflected in the dark glass. A strand of my hair had fallen loose. It hung down one side—my bad side, the burned side. I put down the velvet boater and caught up the hair, twisting it to the back of my head and pinning it. Quickly, I licked my fingers and smoothed down the loose hairs on either side of my head. It had been a long day, and I wasn't looking my best. *Still, it could be worse,* I said to myself. And then—I don't know why—I brought both hands to my mouth and blew my reflection a kiss.

Through the glass, I saw a man walking toward the shop. Had he seen my foolishness? Did he think I'd blown the kiss to him? God in heaven, was he coming this way?

Panic swept over me. Had I locked the door? It wasn't so late, just past seven, but I was alone. I was a woman and I was alone and the streets were empty. There was money in the register, the day's receipts. Would he be after that—or something more horrible? I hurried to the door. Freyda had pulled down the window shade and turned the CLOSED sign to the street. But after she had left, had I locked the door behind her? Had I remembered to lock it?

I grabbed hold of the doorknob at the same time the man on the other side twisted it. I could feel the pull of us against each other, the collision of our opposing desires. He wanted to come in; I wanted to keep him out.

The door held. I had remembered to lock it. Thanks be to God, I had remembered to lock the door after Freyda left.

I waited, silently, breathing in and out. Then I heard a tapping on the door. And a voice.

"Essie? S'me, Jimmy."

"Jimmy?" I said.

My fingers were like clumsy drunks as I fumbled with the lock. I couldn't remember which way to turn it. It seemed stuck in both directions. Finally I got the door open, and there he was, large as life, smiling.

"Jimmy Eagan!" I said.

"At your service," he said, and tipped his bowler hat to me. Hat honor, from Jimmy Eagan.

He came in then, and looked all around, and let out a long, low whistle. "The nicest hat shop I've ever seen," he said. "How'd you get the money for it, Ess?"

"*Nu*, from the charities." I finished wiping off the cutting table, keeping myself busy while I talked. "They collected money after the fire and gave it out to all the girls. Even for the girls who died, their families got something."

"Why the name?" he asked, pointing to the door.

"The Merry Widow?" I shrugged. "It was my signature hat, when I first opened. The one I put in the window. The one that got me my first customers. And . . . I don't know. There's just something about that hat that I like. It's hard to explain exactly."

"I just wondered," said Jimmy, "if you'd gotten married and lost a husband since I saw you last."

"In a year's time?" I said. "No, Jimmy. I've been a little too busy with the shop." It was my whole life. Every minute I was awake I spent here.

"Not married, then?" he asked.

"No, not married," I said. "No marriage for me. Not ever." I turned my head and pointed to the burned side of my face. Some things, I'd learned — well, it's just best to put them right on the table.

"Aw, it's not so much, Ess," he said softly. "It

doesn't change—you're still every bit as beautiful, you know."

"What a horrible liar you are," I said, smiling. His warm, brown eyes, his crooked nose with the bump, his big smile—they were all the same, all as if no time had gone by. "But you, you must be married by now."

"Nope," he said. "I took your advice."

I didn't know what he meant, and my face must have showed it.

He hooked his thumbs in his vest pockets. "I made up my own goddamn mind."

"Oh," I said, but couldn't think of anything else to say. I was just so glad he was here. I felt the fullness of his return, the warm weight of it; a small pocket of emptiness in my heart filled.

"How's your mother?" he asked.

"As strong as ever. Not working at the bakery anymore. She missed too much work after the fire taking care of me, so they let her go. She doesn't mind, though. And Saulie's managed to stay out of jail. He's still in school, and he even helps me with deliveries." I was happy to have good news to tell. Enough with the black thoughts and sad events.

"Your mother! She is one tough old bird," he said, and then stopped and thought for a minute. "I came to see you in the hospital. She asked me to leave." He frowned. "She was very kind about it, but she insisted. She didn't want me to see you."

"Oh," I said again. "She never told me that." It was hard to go back to those days. My mind didn't want to. "I was in the hospital for a long time." I thought back to the weeks on the ward. The screaming. The pain. The light slanting through the window. And the needle. "Those were bad days for me. I'm glad you didn't see me then."

"I'm sorry you suffered," said Jimmy. He reached out his hand and took hold of mine. My crippled hand. He turned it over and looked at it. He uncurled the fingers, feeling the scar that ran deep along the palm.

"Broken," I said. "And sliced open, when I slid down the elevator cable. There were things cut inside — tendons and nerves — that can't be fixed."

"You were brave," he said. "Brave and smart."

"Lucky, really."

"They should have hung those bastards," he said quietly.

"Enough," I said. After the fire, it was all money and legal arguments and written testimony and talk. None of it had anything to do with the girls who had died. One hundred and forty six of them. Yetta Goldstein. Ida Brodsky. Anna Altman. Albina Caruso. The names marched through my head like soldiers going off to war. And always they ended with the name that nobody knew, the one who was buried in an unvisited grave marked with a silver plate: *This casket contains a victim of the Asch building fire. March 25, 1911.*

I said her name. Waiting to cross a street at the end of the day. Sitting on a park bench. Climbing the stairs to the three-bedroom apartment where Mama and Saulie and I now lived. I would say her name out loud. *Dorothy Harriet Camille Arnold.*

Because I think it must be terrible to be lost, but so much worse to be forgotten.

In our new apartment that has no memories of Zelda, Mama and I have put her boots by the door. On a clean square of newspaper that Mama changes every day, her boots sit, reminding us. We find ways to talk about her. We say her name every day. Mama and me, we talk together about the little girl we both loved.

"Essie?" Jimmy said, stooping a little to peer into my face. "You look lost in thought."

"No," I said, smiling at him. "Not lost. Found."

A church bell rang the half hour. "May I walk you home?" he asked.

"Saulie comes for me. He should be here any minute."

"Well, then." Jimmy picked up the black velvet boater and held it out to me. "Is this the one you're wearing home?" he asked.

I took the hat from him, my new best seller, and pinned it on my head. It took me a few minutes to get it straight because of my crippled hand. When I had it just right, the bell over the door rang and Saulie walked in.

"Look at you!" said Jimmy, holding out his hand to shake Saulie's. "Have you grown a foot since I saw you last?"

"Well, look what the cat drug in," said Saulie, smiling and shaking Jimmy's hand in the easy way that men do. He was as tall as Jimmy, but still not as broad. "Are you harassing my sister?"

"Trying to. But she won't have anything to do with me."

"Well, she's the smart one in the family, all right," said Saulie. They talked then, about what they'd been up to, and whether the Giants would win the pennant again this year—"and what about that Rube Marquard, he turned out to be some pitcher, after all. Worth every damn penny they paid for him, I'll tell you what."

I finished clearing off the tables, locked up the day's receipts in the back room safe, and turned off the electric lights, listening to the hum of Jimmy and Saulie's talk—not so much the words, just the easy rise and fall of it.

"All ready, Ess?" asked Saulie when I came to stand beside him. I nodded my head, and we all walked out the door together. I locked up the shop, my eyes resting for just a moment on the bizarre hat that sat, front and center, in the display window. I was starting to gain a reputation for originality that was spreading all the way uptown. But I might have gone too far with this one. Tomorrow, I would ask Freyda what she thought.

"Well, I should be going," said Jimmy. "Good night to you both." He touched his hand to the brim of his hat.

"You could come with," I said. "If you had a mind to. We could get a cup of coffee, or even something to eat."

Jimmy looked at me and smiled. He turned to my brother. "Mr. Rosenfeld?"

Saulie shrugged. "So long as Essie's paying, it's

okay with me."

"My treat," said Jimmy. "Where should we go?"

"Let's just wander," I said. "It's a nice night. We'll find someplace, I'm sure."

With my right hand I took Saulie's arm, and with my left hand, the crippled one, I took Jimmy's. The night was warm. The air was soft and forgiving. We began to walk.

Chapter 18

THE LETTER IN MY HAND IS LIGHTER THAN A BIRD. I think about offering it up to the wind that barrels up Fifth Avenue. It's a gusty, wild day in March. If I let the wind snatch up the letter, it might make it all the way uptown to 79th Street. The wind, after all, is invisible and strong.

That would be an act of fatalism, I say to myself. I remember explaining to Zelda what fatalism is. It had been in that same book, the one that talked of free will.

"Fatalism," I had said to her, "is when you don't bother to do anything to make your life better because it's all in God's hands anyway. You just let God decide everything and you wait to see what happens."

Zelda had wrinkled up her nose and shook her head. "God don't work like that," she had said.

I place the letter in the flat palm of my good hand and hold it up, like an offering to God. The handwriting on the envelope is peculiar, the *t*'s like church spires, each *y* a trampled snake. The wind plays with the corners of the letter, turning it a little, until it jumps up and makes a break for it.

I grab with both hands and get it back. Here's the truth: I'm no fatalist and never was. I believe in *doing*. In the year since the fire, I'd spent hours at Harriet's apartment going through her things. Bit

233

by bit, I'd taken her clothes and given them away. The hatpins and trinkets, I pawned and gave the money to the workers union. The letters from Italy, the ones from the lover who left her, I burned.

After that, I swept and dusted. I shook out the heavy curtains. I raked out the stove. I made sure all the gas jets were off. I pounded the sofa pillows and straightened the rug. And then I left the key on the kitchen table and walked out for the last time.

The letter in my hand is all that I have left. I've carried it with me now for months, not sure what to do with it. Not sure what is right and what is wrong. Not sure what Harriet would have wanted. After all, I'd only known her for a few weeks. But I hoped that somehow a sign would be given to me, telling me what to do.

God don't work like that.

I don't know if the dead speak from beyond the grave. I know that I hear Zelda's voice inside my head every day. I know that I can be walking down the street and catch a bit of a song, or there's a piano playing somewhere, or someone laughs, and then it's like she's never left me.

I hold the letter in my hands, and I *do* know what Harriet would have wanted. She would have wanted to give comfort. She would have done her best. She would have lived.

I reach out with my claw hand and pull the handle on the mailbox. The painted metal groans. I peer into the slot. It's a black hole stuffed with nothing. Carefully, I place the letter on the edge of the darkness. And then I let go, and it falls and falls and falls.

March 24

My Very Dearest John,

How can I even begin to say how sorry I am for the sadness I've caused you and Mother and Father and everyone in the family? I know that my actions have brought you pain, and for that I am more sorry than words can say. Will you believe me when I tell you that I had to leave? Will you forgive me?

I am well, John. Truly and wholly well. Please stop your worrying, and please, please stop searching. I have found a happy life. I have friends who are dear to me. I have work—if you can believe it! And I have music in my life, a piano that I play every day. I do! You know I could never live without my music.

Someday, we will meet again in heaven. I'm looking forward to that! You'll tease me about my hat—do they wear hats in heaven, I wonder—and I'll call you Johnny Jump-up and it will be jolly and like old times without any of this sadness and worry. I'll see you in the great beyond, Johnny my boy, and until then, I am ever and forever
Your own darling sister,
Dorothy

Author's Note

On January 26, 1911, the lead headline on the front page of *The New York Times* read: NIECE OF PECKHAM STRANGELY MISSING.

The news article told how Dorothy Harriet Camille Arnold, the twenty-five-year-old daughter of a wealthy perfume importer with high social standing, and the niece of a former Supreme Court justice, had disappeared. She left her family home at 108 East 79th Street the morning of December 12, 1910, and walked down Fifth Avenue to shop for a dress for her sister's coming-out party. Along the way, she made two stops: she bought a box of chocolates at Park & Tilford's grocery on 59th Street and she bought a book, *Engaged Girl Sketches*, at Brentano's on the corner of 5th and 27th. Outside the bookstore, she ran into a friend, and they talked about various topics of interest to them, including an upcoming party they would both attend. The friend later reported that Dorothy had seemed to be in good spirits.

But she was never seen again. She disappeared in broad daylight, and no trace of her was ever found—despite the efforts of thousands of police officers, private detectives from the famous Pinkerton Detective Agency, and concerned citizens. Dorothy Arnold had vanished.

The nation was gripped by the story. It was front-page news every day for months, and stories

236

of reported sightings of Dorothy Arnold continued for years, long after the police had placed the disappearance in their cold case file.

Many unusual twists and turns to the story emerged during the months of reporting following Dorothy's disappearance. The first odd fact was that the Arnold family had waited six weeks to report their daughter's disappearance to the police. Although Dorothy didn't return home from her walk on December 12, 1910, the Arnolds didn't notify the police until January 25, 1911. Instead, they had hired an army of Pinkerton detectives to try to locate Dorothy. The press assumed there was some scandal that the family was trying to conceal. They dug deeper and found plenty to feed the gossip-hungry readership of New York — and the whole world.

Among other things, it was revealed in the papers that Dorothy had a secret lover: a jowly, forty-year-old bachelor named George ("Junior") Griscom, Jr., who still lived with his parents in Pittsburgh. Most shockingly, in September of 1910, Dorothy had spent a week in Boston with Griscom, unchaperoned. At the end of that week, she had pawned five hundred dollars worth of jewelry for sixty dollars. Some have speculated that Dorothy might have become pregnant during this trip to Boston.

It was also revealed that Dorothy had dreams of becoming a writer and that she had secretly rented a post office box where she received rejection letters for the stories she submitted to magazines. She had begged her father to allow her to keep an apartment in Greenwich Village so that she could pursue her writing, but her father had refused, fearing scandal.

Following the disappearance, Dorothy's oldest brother, John, and their mother traveled to Florence, Italy, in January, 1911, to question Griscom, who was vacationing there with his parents. John demanded that Griscom hand over letters he had received from Dorothy. There was a struggle, and Griscom eventually gave John several letters, but these letters were never turned over to the police. The Arnolds insisted that there was nothing of importance in the letters and that they had burned them.

Years later, on April 8, 1921, while speaking in a lecture hall to an audience of listeners, Police Captain John H. Ayers, head of the Bureau of Missing Persons in New York City, declared that the Dorothy Arnold case had, in fact, been solved by the police department. He said, "All I can say is that it [the Arnold case] has been solved by the department. Dorothy Arnold is no longer listed as a missing person. I probably shouldn't have mentioned the case, as it is a strictly confidential one in the department." This statement, which was vehemently denied by the Arnold family, fueled more speculation that the fate of the missing heiress was known, but that the family chose to keep it a secret because of some unreported scandal.

Just two months after the news of Dorothy's

disappearance first hit the papers, a different story grabbed the headlines. On March 26, 1911, the front page of *The New York Times* ran a four-column headline: 141 MEN AND GIRLS DIE IN WAIST FACTORY FIRE; TRAPPED HIGH UP IN WASHINGTON PLACE BUILDING; STREET STREWN WITH BODIES; PILES OF DEAD INSIDE.

The newspaper went on to report that on the warm spring afternoon of March 25, 1911, a fire broke out on the eighth floor of the Triangle Waist Company, a factory that occupied the eighth, ninth, and tenth floors of the Asch Building on the corner of Washington Place and Greene Street in New York City. About five hundred people worked at the Triangle—most of them teenage girls and women—sewing ready-to-wear shirtwaists, a type of ladies' blouse that was popular at the time.

The Triangle was a typical factory of the era: it worked its employees hard, six days a week, in crowded rooms with unsafe conditions for starvation wages. Girls were dismissed on the spot for talking, humming, having unclean hands, or getting sick. Managers regularly locked the doors to keep the girls in and the union organizers out. There was no fire alarm system, no sprinkler system, and the single fire escape ended at the second floor.

Ensuring worker safety in 1911 America was a two-headed problem. First, there weren't enough laws on the books that sought to minimize the risk to workers. For example, there was no law requiring sprinkler systems in New York City factories;

nor was there a law requiring fire drills or fire escapes. A loophole in one law allowed factory owners to dangerously overcrowd a factory floor — as long as the factory's ceiling was high enough.

Second, there was very little effort to enforce the few laws and regulations that did exist. Factory bosses often bribed fire inspectors, and there weren't enough fire inspectors — honest or other-wise — to adequately monitor the working conditions in the factories.

When the fire broke out at the Triangle, just minutes before closing time, many of the workers on the eighth floor were able to escape because they were the first to know of the danger. Those in the executive offices on the tenth floor — the facto-ry owners, switchboard operators, secretaries, cashiers, bookkeepers, and garment pressers — escaped with just one casualty because they received an early telephone warning from the eighth floor. But nobody warned the girls on the ninth floor. By the time they understood that the building was on fire, several key escape routes had been cut off: the narrow Greene Street stairway was cut off by fire; the Washington Place stairway was locked; the overheated elevator tracks were nearly melted to the point of nonfunction, and the rusted fire escape would soon be so burdened with terrified girls that it would peel away from the building and collapse, plunging dozens of girls to their deaths.

With no way out, the girls on the ninth floor turned to the floor-to-ceiling windows that lined the walls overlooking Washington Place and Greene Street. The glass had been blown out by the heat of the fire so that the windows were wide open to the outside world.

Dozens of girls jumped. They fell eighty feet and landed on the sidewalk. An enormous crowd had gathered outside the burning building, and stunned onlookers watched as the girls, some of them as young as fourteen, fell to the ground and lay in a broken heap on the sidewalk.

One hundred and forty six people died in the Triangle Shirtwaist Factory fire. It took weeks for authorities and family members to identify the bodies. In the end, seven bodies remained unidentified. The remains of those bodies are buried in the Evergreens Cemetery in Brooklyn, marked by a small stone monument. To this day, no one knows the names of those who lie buried there. There is no evidence to prove that Dorothy Arnold died in the Triangle fire; likewise, there's no proof that she didn't.

In writing this novel, I've remained as faithful as possible to the facts of these two stories—the missing heiress and the Triangle fire tragedy—while allowing myself to imagine how these two stories might have intersected. In *Lost*, the police description of Dorothy Arnold that Essie finds posted in The Tombs is the actual one mailed to the police of nearly every city and many towns across the country in 1911. The article entitled "Lost" that Essie reads in the newspaper appeared in the March 12, 1911, edition of *The New York Times*. Although this book is a work of fiction, there is nothing within these pages that I know to contradict the truth. But as with so many pieces of our histories—private and public, individual and collective—there are things that we will simply never know

—Jacqueline Davies, September 2008

JACQUELINE DAVIES